An Exciting and Adventurous way to view History

Book Four of the

Saving History Series

Loose

Ends

Robert Starnes

Robert Starnes

Published by Starnes Books LLC
Edited by Carpenter Editing Services, LLC

ISBN: 978-1-7325803-8-1 (sc)
ISBN: 978-1-7325803-9-8 (e)
ISBN: 978-1-7347928-6-7 (hc)

Library of Congress Control Number:2019919103

Printed in the United States of America
First Printing 2019

Dedication

I would like to take the time to dedicate this installment of the *Saving History Series, Loose Ends,* to everyone who is living with any form of ASD (Autism Spectrum Disorder) on a daily basis. As someone who is living with Asperger's, I can understand how difficult things are for us at times. I can also see how things are difficult for those around us as well. I believe that we are born special for a reason, so I challenge everyone to find their reason. Don't let someone tell you that you can't do something because of your ASD. You can prove them wrong, because I know you can do anything you set your perfect, genius mind to. We will change the world, we just have to try regardless of what others say.

Now I want to also dedicate this installment to anyone living with a reading disorder, such as Dyslexia, like myself. Reading has always been very hard for me at a young age, but I also was not aware I had Dyslexia and ASD. Because I was made fun of for my reading slow, I chose not to read. I know I missed out on so many great books because of the choice I made, because of what others thought of me. I'm begging you all to ignore anyone who says anything about your reading skills and keep reading. One day you could be an Author, Editor, or even a Publisher. You control your future, unlike the characters of the *Saving History Series,* so pick up a book and read at your own pace. The goal of reading is just to relax and enjoy another world. Trust me, you will be surprised how much you actually love to read, and even how much you can improve without even trying.

We are all the same, yet different at the same time, but we are all people. I can't wait to read some of your works in the future. You are never alone, you all always have me on your side.

Contents

Prologue: Leaders Unite

Now that the Council and the remaining leaders are certain that a time ripple has caught up with them causing King Preston to vanish, they all agree with Fisher of the Aquarians, that they all do need to work together. Although they are not truly upset by the mention of someone vanishing, even a King, but deep down inside they do seem to have a feeling that they are not missing much.

"King Payton, will you still be requiring your very large payment for your assistance?" Fisher asks the now King of the Embers.

"If it involves getting my brother back, then no payment is required. That was his requirement, not mine," King Payton replies to Fisher. "You may not remember my brother, and if you do, you may not even like him, but he is still my family. He's my brother. I will do whatever I can to get my family back."

"Thank you, your Highness. We will all do what we can to correct ALL of history, so we can have our previous timeline back in place, the one with your brother in it as well," the Council leader conveys to the new King.

"Now that we are very aware of what we are up against, I suggest we each do what we need to do, or send for whoever we need to, in order to create a plan to save our past, and possible future," Fisher is addressing the room now. "I know that time is not something we have on our side right now, and it actually is completely against us, and with none to spare, I will need to send for the help we can provide.”

“Same here,” replies the new King of the Embers.

“Rose and I will be all you will need from the Fairley Folk. We are all equally equipped and skilled just the same,” Emma speaks to the Council leader.

“Tell us what we are all missing, once we have everyone in place, and we will surely be able to make it happen,” Council leader reassures them all. “Now, why don’t you all do what you need to do, and we can reconvene in two days?”

“As long as we have two days,” King Payton mouths under his breath sadly, thinking of his lost brother, Preston.

“Until then, please be careful, and if anything changes, please let the Council know, so they can inform us remaining leaders of the situation,” Fisher instructs the team, as it has now been formed. “Safe travels and safe return, see everyone in two days.”

Chapter 1

Who Won?

As Jax makes his way from the home he once had with the Believers in North Zulch, he swears he can feel a faint call from Kenzie saying, *Jax, we should have listened to you.* Of course, he is not sure if it is real or just what he expects to hear from them, Ian and Kenzie. He does not have much faith that they will wait for his return before going into Maria's room to look around, even after they said they would wait for him.

Jax could feel the fear in Kenzie's last thoughts to him about Maria having taken Brayden and Connor away from the school. He still can't believe that Maria, of all people, being the Head of the Believers, would do something like that. "She is the head of the Believers. No matter what her reasons, she is breaking every rule of a Believer and the moral codes of being human," Jax talks to himself while driving as fast as he can, without breaking the speed limits or any laws.

He does not have to drive too long down Farm Market road 1452, to Highway 190, until he reaches Interstate 45 South towards Houston. From there he knows his drive will be almost two and a half hours with traffic. He may not even be close to Houston yet, but he knows there is always traffic in Houston, especially at the time of day he will be arriving downtown at the school.

Kenzie, can you hear me? Jax continues to try to make some kind of contact with her mind as he drives to give him something to do and to make sure they are okay. But he receives no reply. He will continue to repeat trying to connect with her mind until she answers, or he gets to school and finds them. Right now, all he can do is drive and keep trying to contact Kenzie.

***

Maria leaves Mason standing there, alone in the conference room, the one they were using in the Control room. As she begins her exit of the Control room, she stops at the door. Her phone seems to be buzzing in her pocket, so she reaches for it to see what's so important. Upon retrieving her phone from her pocket, she reads a message on her locked screen that reads, "Room Alarm Tripped." That message seems to make her eyes brighten up like the northern star in the night sky at dusk, and a small smile shoots across her hardened face.

"I knew I would catch the other two, once they found out that they were not actually hearing me, nor watching me down in the school lobby. It funny how Brayden was right about Ian and Kenzie going right up to my room looking for him and Connor. Even though we have them here with us now, I do wonder what took them so long before going into my room. Could it have been due to moral issues, or maybe it is because Jax would not allow them. Either way, I cannot wait to have them as well to add to our collection," Maria says to herself, softly. "Now I just need to get back before anyone notices they are missing as well as the ring from Kayla."

Maria makes her way out of the Control room closing the door behind her. She makes sure not to be too fast or too loud to draw any undue attention to herself from Mason or anyone else in the room. This is one new development that she wants to keep to herself for as long as she can, or at least until she can confirm it is who she believes she has trapped in her room.

She makes her way down the hallway with a little more pep in her step that is noticed by one of the guards.

"You must have somewhere important to be, ma'am," the guard sounds off to Maria.

Caught off guard, Maria replies, "Excuse me?"

"Well, it's just that you seem to be much happier leaving here that when you first arrived, and you are also moving at a much faster pace. You would think you were running to watch an enemy's house burn to the ground while blocking the roads so the fire trucks couldn't get to it in time," the guard conveys some humor.

"Oh, no. I mean, yes, I am in a hurry. I have to get back to work before people notice I'm gone. That's why I'm walking so fast."

"Yes, ma'am. Well, be safe out there on the streets. I hear traffic is something terrible today in Houston."

"It's Houston, dear. Traffic is always horrible every day, but I will do my best," Maria ends their conversation, so she may exit the building to get to her car and begin her drive to the school in downtown Houston. She knows it's going to take her about two and a half hours to get from Woodville to downtown Houston with all the traffic.

As Maria takes her seat in the driver's side of the car, all she can think of is the importance of her finding those two in her room, but she also knows it could be Jax himself. She would prefer Kenzie and Ian, but she would take Jax just as well. She knows that if she has Jax, then none of the children, Kenzie, Ian, Connor, nor Brayden would allow anything to happen to him, and they would do exactly what she and Mason asked them to do. So, for her, it would be a win-win scenario either way.

Maria takes highway 190 from Woodville, but unlike Jax, she is not one to obey the posted speed limit signs or laws. So even though she and Jax have the exact same distance and time to travel, and they have left at the same time, without the other knowing, Maria looks to be the first to arrive at the school.

***

Kayla does not fight against her new body guest, the special visitor that is helping her and the others by using their bodies at times, and allows him to lead her to Mason's office. She keeps thinking this is a very bad idea, but her visitor assures her otherwise. He repeatedly tells her that they are going to be fine, because Mason and Maria are in their meeting, as she already knows, so the coast is clear.

The pair of them head down the hall towards Mason's office, in Kayla's body of course. It does not take them long to reach his office, as it is not too far from her room. He likes to be as close as possible to her at all times.

Now that they are standing in front of his office door, Kayla asks her company, "Now what?"

"Mason is so convinced no one would ever betray him, even after his traitor was revealed, great job by the way, he still leaves his office door unlocked," The visiting History student, from another place and time, replies while reaching for the door knob and giving it a quick turn.

To Kayla's surprise, the door is indeed unlocked. She, or they, push the door open to Mason's office and quickly walked in and shut the door behind them.

"Figures he would have such a large office, and just look at all of those books. There must be over a thousand of them. Why in the world does he need this huge oak desk? Who does he think he is, the President of the United States?" Kayla is talking to her partner-in-crime out loud at the moment.

"To his followers, he might as well be the President. Now, we need to get back to business here. Do you mind if I take control over your body again?"

"Fine, but let's be quick. I really don't want to get caught in here."

He takes control over Kayla's body and leads her over to Mason's office safe. The same safe he placed the ring in, the one Kayla gives Ian on his eighteenth birthday, or did give it to him already. Without hesitation, Kayla's hand moves to the keypad on the door of the safe and begins to press in a six-digit code. The light on the safe turns from red to green, letting them both know the safe is unlocked.

"How do you know the code to his safe?" Kayla's asks her companion.

"History, remember?"

"I forgot. Well, what are we getting out of here that is more important than my safety?"

"Trust me, you will soon find out!"

As Kayla's hand turns the handle to the unlocked safe and gives it a quick pull, she notices right off the bat what they are there to take. "We are here for Ian's ring."

"I told you, you would know soon enough. Now, we need to get the ring and get out of here. NOW!"

"What are those?"

"What are you referring to?"

"Why would Mason have a lock of hair, a journal, some old coins, and who is that in that old picture?"

"I'm sorry, but I can't tell you about those things. We are only here for the ring. The less you know about the future the better. We can't mess up the future. We just need to get it back on the right path."

"Fine, whatever you say. This is your mission anyway. So, are we ready to get the ring and go to my room now?"

"Yes, now grab the ring and close the safe door and press in the code again to lock it back. We need to be going, if my memory serves me correctly."

Kayla grabs the silver ring Alexis gave her to give to Ian on his eighteenth birthday. This must mean she will be able to give it to him again. But as soon as she touches the ring, she freezes.

Kayla? What's going on? Why can't I speak with your voice, and why are you just standing here? Kayla's body occupant thinks to her, as he is unable to speak out loud with her own voice.

***

Ian is back in his memory of the skiing trip he took with his fictional family. It is the memory where he has an older brother, Pete, a niece, Kourtney, a little brother, John Dock, and little sister, Ashley. He is right back at the point where Pete dropped two large bags at his feet. They are unloading the car after just getting to the cabin and before they can go to the slopes. This is the same dream he was torn away from to be led to the memory of Sebastian and Grayson's fight.

Ian bends down to pick up at least one of the oversized bags Pete has left at his feet, but before he has time to retrieve it and head into the cabin, the cabin and his family disappear again. Ian is back in the white room he knows all too well. He knows this is the same room Junior used to communicate with him, before he was wiped from the future, with Kayla erasing herself from History.

Junior? Can this really be you? Jax says he believes it is you, Ian thinks to anyone at this moment. He is not really sure what to expect.

Yes, Ian. It is me, Junior. I am here with you, but right now you are in a bad situation that I'm not sure I can help you get out of.

What are you talking about? I'm with my family. I am just fine.

No, Ian, you are not fine. You and Kenzie are in big trouble right now. You have both been knocked out by a sleeping spell. You are both asleep in Maria's room. We have to find a way to wake you up before she gets here!

I don't understand. I feel fine. I'm happy here. Why would I want to leave?

Ian, this is not your life, or even your true actual memory. This is just a dream of what you wish life could have been for you, but it's all fake. You did go skiing, but it was just you, John and Donna, your mom and dad. You have no siblings or even a niece. You are an only child. Ian, you have to remember!

Why? Why do I have to remember? Why can't I just stay here?

You have to WAKE UP and get out of Maria's room. NOW! If not for you, then think about Kenzie. She is stuck in here with you! WAKE UP!

***

Jax makes his two-and-a-half-hour drive from North Zulch in only two hours, faster than he anticipated. He does not take the time to park his car in the parking garage of the school, but instead he parks right in front of the front doors.

He jumps out of the car and bursts through the front doors and ignores the concierge, on a mad dash to the elevators. He is in such a hurry that he does not recognize another student yelling out his name.

"Jax! Can I speak to you for a minute?" The student finally catches Jax's attention.

"Sorry, but I don't have time to talk at the moment. Can it wait until later?" Jax replies to the student.

"Okay, but it's about class," the student replies.

"Then you will be fine," Jax concludes their conversation.

Jax jumps into the elevator as soon as the doors open, as he had pressed the call button as soon as he arrived in the elevator lobby. Once he is alone in the elevator, he presses the button for the fourteenth floor, as that is the floor for the heads of the faculty, like Maria.

Jax has to endure the hum of the elevator belts and the tick of the digital clock counting the floors as they pass them. The anticipation is ripping him up inside. He knows he has to find Ian and Kenzie before Maria does. He knows the first place he must look is her room, since he has a feeling they did not wait for him to get back before they went into her room, like he suggested. If they are in her room, he has to get them out before she can get them, if they are to be safe. Then sounds the loud 'ding,' letting him know he has made it to the fourteenth floor.

As quick as the elevator doors can open, Jax slides between and begins his rush to Maria's room, 1402. He reaches her door, grabs the door knob and gives it a twist, and he finds it unlocked. He pushes open her door and finds…

***

Maria skids to a stop at the parking garage entrance, knowing she has already lost precious time due to her being stopped and given a ticket for speeding on her way through Houston. She knows the speed limit signs are there for a reason, and she should have obeyed them. Now, she will have to suffer the consequences.

Once she was able to get into the parking garage and park her car, on the third floor, which was the first level with an open spot, she took it. She has her own spot on the first floor, but it seems that someone has parked in it during her absence. She knows she does not have time to deal with that right now, she needs to get to her room. She gets out of her new parking spot and makes a quick step to the elevators in the garage to take her down to the ground level of the structure.

She has taken the elevator from the third floor to the ground floor in the parking garage, and as she steps up to the door, she swipes her card for access, but it is not working for some reason. She continues to try again, but still no access. By this time, Maria is furious that she does not have access to the building. She is beginning to worry if she has been found out about working with Mason.

Maria plays it cool and presses the intercom button to get the concierge.

"Yes, may I help you?" The voice comes from the speaker of the concierge on duty for the evening.

"I am Maria, Head of the Believers, and I reside in unit 1402, and my access card is not working. You can start by buzzing me in and having me a working access card and key to my room, before I make it to your desk in the lobby. Do I make myself clear?" Maria is still trying to sound the same way she always would, as if she suspects nothing at the moment.

"Yes, ma'am! Right away! I'm not sure why your card is not working, but I'm sure it's just a glitch in the system. Your new card and key will be ready as soon as you make it to my desk," the concierge speaks through the speaker as Maria hears the doors being buzzed unlocked for her access.

Maria takes the door and swings it open to make her way to the concierge's desk. "My new card and key, please!"

"Yes, ma'am. Here you go. So sorry about the mix up at the exterior door. I'll make sure it won't happen again," the on-duty concierge replies as she hands Maria her new access card and room key.

"Thank you," Maria spouts back to the, now upset, concierge who picked the wrong shift to switch with a coworker. Maria snatches the card and key out of her hand.

Maria turns and makes a rush for the elevators. As soon as she reaches them, she presses the up button and has to wait for one of the three elevators that is currently working this evening, which looks to be coming from the Sky Lounge floor.

The elevator stops for her in the lobby, the doors open, and she enters with only one thing on her mind now. Who is she going to catch in her room? So, she presses the button with the fourteen on it, for her floor. "I can't wait to see who I have caught this time!"

The elevator stops on the fourteenth floor, with a loud 'ding,' and Maria quickly steps out and makes her way down to her room door. Upon arrival, she does not notice anything unusual about it, so she puts in her key, unlocks the door, grabs the handle, and pushes the door open to find…

Chapter 2

Passed Out?

Kayla, standing silently in front of Mason's open office safe, with the ring she gives to Ian on his eighteenth birthday, which is really from Alexis, is wondering why she is still standing there. She does not realize it, but she has snapped back to reality, suddenly, and is a bit confused.

"Why, is the safe open and why are we still here?" she asks of her body companion, but she receives no reply. "Hello? What do we do now? This is your mission not mine, remember?"

With nothing in response except her own thoughts and voice, in a panic she slams the safe door shut, then twists the safe handle until the lights on the safe turn red, letting her know that the safe is locked again. Now that she has the ring and the safe is locked, she just needs to get out of Mason's office without being seen. She makes a turn for the office door and a quick dash to it, but before she can make it to the door, she hears Mason's voice outside of it. *Now what do I do?* she thinks to herself.

I'm so glad you are awake now, Kayla. I don't know what happened to you, but now is not the time for us to figure that out. May I please have control back and quickly?

Kayla, excited to have her body invader back, does as he ask and gives him full control over her body.

Now, in control of Kayla, the body hopping History student runs as fast as they can over to Mason's oversized oak desk, and work their way under it. They pull his desk chair up to the desk to close them in and out of sight. The desk is so grand, they have plenty of room underneath it. *We should be safe here, as long as Mason does not sit down, or drop anything,* he thinks to Kayla.

And if that happens? Then what?

One thing at a time. Now let's just listen.

As Mason enters his office, shutting his door behind him, the conversation he was having outside in the hall has ended.

"I'm telling you that I don't trust Maria. She has something going on that does not include nor concerns us, and that worries me," Mason tells himself.

"Don't worry about Maria. I can handle her. I just need you to keep me in the loop for anything changing in the future history. Do you understand? This will be the only way for us to succeed," Mason replies back to himself.

"Yes, I understand. But you also must know that a time ripple may take days, weeks, or maybe even years, before I can see it and determine if it changes anything, which is even if I see it at all. Time ripples can be small at the time, I won't see them, but they could have a major impact in the far future. You understand this, correct?"

"I know, but just do your best and come back when you know more," Mason ends his conversation with himself. Now that he is no longer talking to himself, he turns to his office door to exit, then stops and makes a quick turn towards his office desk. Mason makes his way towards his desk now, instead of his office door.

Oh no! He's coming over to the desk. What do we do? Kayla thinks to her body partner frantically.

Nothing, yet. Let's see what he does first.

Mason walks around to the backside of his desk and places his hand upon the back of his desk chair. With little hesitation, he pulls back his chair, but only enough for him to be able to open the top drawer of the desk. Once the chair is far enough away from the desk for him to accomplish his goal, Mason reaches down, pulls the desk drawer open and grabs something from it, then closes it, while pushing his desk chair back up against the desk. Mason does not leave, but just stands there behind the desk.

His stance behind his office chair is making Kayla very anxious. She just has a feeling he knows she is under his desk.

No, he doesn't, Kayla. Please relax, before you give our position away.

Kayla complies with the instructions of the words from the calmer side of herself, at this time, and relaxes.

After Kayla sweats for a few seconds, which seems more like a few hours to her, Mason turns again and walks for his office door. As Mason leaves his desk, Kayla is able to relax more, for the first time, since before Mason walked into his office.

Mason reaches the office door, opens it and walks through it, closing it behind him. They are in the all-clear now that Mason has left the room.

Kayla and her calmer side are finally alone. Knowing they can't leave his office at this very moment, they remain under his desk. *So, what happened to you earlier? Where did you go, and why did you leave me here alone?* she thinks to her body partner.

I'm sorry that I left you, but when you grabbed the ring, you froze. I was going to ask you the same thing as to what happened to you at that moment, but I was just glad to be back. When you froze, our connection was severed, and I was pulled somewhere else for a moment. So, what happened to you when you touched the ring?

I honestly don't know what you are talking about. As soon as I grabbed the ring, you were gone. You left me here, alone, to finish your mission. How could you do that to me? You know I didn't want to do this anyway.

You mean you don't remember freezing?

No, I don't know what you are talking about. I didn't freeze, you just left.

Yes, you froze, and then I was pulled away!

Where did you go? Where did you get pulled to? Is that even possible for you to be pulled somewhere?

Before her calm companion answers that question, he decided that enough time has passed for them to make an escape from Mason's office now. *We can talk about that later. Right now, we need to get you out of here and into your room. NOW!*

Without any more thoughts between them, Kayla gives control over her body to the calmer part of herself to get her safely to her room. First, they push Mason's desk chair back far enough for them to climb out from underneath of the massive oak desk, push the chair back, and make their way over to the office door. Once they are positioned in front of the door, Kayla's ear presses up against it, listening to make sure there is no one in the hallway. They want to make a swift exit, and an empty hall would be perfect for them to succeed.

To their relief, the hall sounds silent. Together they take the door knob and open it slowly. As the door is opening, they are peeking through the crack in the door to double check that it is indeed clear, which it is. They make their quick exit from Mason's office, shutting his door behind them, and quickly begin to make their way to Kayla's room.

As they approach her room, they are both excited they were able to pull of the heist without being caught. This time it is Kayla who reaches for the bedroom doorknob and gives it a slight turn and pushes it open. As she has control of her body now, she enters her room and then suddenly is frozen with fear, for Mason is standing there, in her room waiting for her.

"Ah, there you are. Where have you been? I thought I told you to go straight to your room," Mason greets Kayla.

***

…to Jax's dismay, Maria's room is empty. There is no sign of Ian, Kenzie, or Maria in her room. *Am I too late?* Jax wonders to himself.

***

…her room is empty. There are no signs of Ian, Kenzie, or Jax there. *How can this be possible?* Maria thinks in anger to herself. *No one has ever escaped my traps before.*

***

Ian begins to wake up from the sleep spell put on him and Kenzie, the one released upon them as they broke into Maria's room. They were there to search for any clues as to where she may have taken Brayden and

Connor, since she captured them breaking into her room and has taken them off school campus. Ian and Kenzie did not have enough time to find anything out, as Maria's spell knocked them out as soon as they entered her room before they could search or escape. The last thing Ian remembers is waving Kenzie to come in to Maria's room, as they were breaking into it to find Brayden and Connor, so he is surprised to be waking up in his own bed in his own room and seeing Kenzie in Brayden's bed.

"Kenzie? Are you awake?"

"Where are we? What happened? Has Maria caught us too?" Kenzie replies back with a load of questions.

"So, you are awake, and you are okay. That's good. Now, I don't think we have been caught because we are in mine and Brayden's room and he is not here, nor Connor, so they are still missing. I don't know how we got here, but we are here just the same. Do you remember anything from when we went to Maria's room?"

"Well, I just remember you waving me to come into her room, but as soon as I walked in, the bedroom door slammed shut. I called your name out and looked over to you, but you were already falling to the floor, asleep. Next thing I know, I'm waking up here."

"Then how in the world did we get here?"

"You tell me! I'm just a kid," Kenzie utters to Ian for some reassurance.

"Sorry. I have no answers for you right now, but I think there may be someone who might have some. Are you really okay? Are you unharmed?"

"Yes, I am unharmed, and I'm fine, just a little shaken. How are you?"

"Good, but I am going to need you to trust me right now, okay? Remember how I think there is someone that may know something about how we got here?"

"Yes, I remember. You just said it."

"Well, I need to go see that girl, River Kate. You were talking to her down in the lobby earlier when we were supposed to be spying on Maria. I have a feeling she may be able to shed some light on our situation."

"How in the world can she help us right now? And why do you even think she can? This is not a crush thing is it? We just woke up from a deep sleep, after breaking into a teacher's room, and you want to go and flirt with a girl?"

"It's not like that at all. I have a feeling that I can't describe, but I believe she can help us. Please, just trust me for a few minutes. I'll be right back."

"Fine. I'll stay here in your room and wait for you to return. But I'm warning you, you better have something more than just a phone number when you return, or I'm going to be mad that I had to wait for you to go make a date."

"I'm not going to make a date. I swear."

"In that case, would you like to know where she is right now?"

"Who?"

"River Kate, silly. I can tell you where she is really quick. She won't even know I am in her head."

"Yes, that would be awesome, and it would save me a lot of time having to look for her."

"River Kate is actually alone, up in the Sky Lounge. Hurry and you will beat the friends she's waiting for to get there."

"Thank you, Kenzie. That's just one floor up. I'll take the stairs to save time, since waiting on the elevator could take too long. Make sure the door locks behind me as I close it and don't open it for anyone, except me. You got it?"

"Got it, boss!"

"I'm not your boss, so don't call me that," Ian tells Kenzie as he walks out his bedroom door, closing it to make sure it locks behind him, before he makes his move over to the stairs. Once he is sure the door to his bedroom is closed and locked, he goes passed the trash chute and to the emergency exit door. He pushes the exit door open which leads into the stairwell.

Ian knows that he will have access to the top floor from the stairwell, which is where the pool, gym, patio, and Sky Lounge are located. He also knows that he has access to the bottom floor, the lobby. He is glad that he is going up instead of down the stairs this time. He has had to take the stairs down from his floor to the lobby, during two false fire alarms so far since he has been at the school. Those were not pleasant times, because he also had to take the stairs back up to his floor as well, each time. Twenty-two flights of stairs, down and back up again, twice.

Ian makes his way up the one flight of stairs to the top floor, opens the emergency exit door, and makes his way into the hallway that leads to the amenities and the elevators. Once he walks past the elevator doors, he turns left and there is a door to the Sky Lounge. Through the small window in the door, he can see River Kate standing next to the pool table that is in the room. She is alone, just as Kenzie said she would be.

As Ian enters the Sky Lounge, River Kate turns to greet him, thinking it is her friends that are on their way up to help her decorate for Ms. Carol's surprise birthday party. She has a stunned look on her face. Shocked to see Ian at the door, she asks, "Hey, Ian. How is Kenzie doing?"

To Ian's surprise, he is curious as to why she would ask such a question about Kenzie. *When did you see River Kate last, Kenzie?* Ian thinks.

The only time I have ever spoken to or seen River Kate was in the lobby when we thought we were listening to Maria. Why?

I'll get back to you, Ian thinks back to Kenzie before answering River Kate's question. "She is doing much better now. Thank you for asking," Ian acknowledges her question.

"Oh, that's good to know. She didn't look so well when I saw you carrying her in the elevator. She was passed out."

"Yes, she was so tired from being up all night studying for a test. She just wore herself out. I tried to tell her that it's just an elementary school, but she wants to make sure she has perfect grades no matter what grade level she is in. Can I ask you a question? When did you see me carrying her again? I've been up all night studying with her, so my time is a bit off as well."

"It was about ten minutes ago. I was coming up here and the elevator stopped on the fourteenth floor. I thought that was odd being a private faculty sleeping floor, but you got on the elevator carrying Kenzie. I tried to talk to you, but it was as if you had no clue who I was. You and Kenzie got off on the twenty-second floor, and now you are here. So, what can I do for you?"

"First, I want to apologize about the elevator incident earlier. Between her passing out and my own exhaustion, I wasn't being respectful to you. And second, I do remember you telling me about this party up here. You said if I was up to it, that I was invited. Is that still an option?"

"It is, but the party does not start for another hour. I am just waiting for some friends to come and help decorate, remember?"

"Yes, I remember. You have friends coming to help you. I remember. So, since I have an hour, I am going to go back down to my room, check on Kenzie and get ready for the party. Is that okay?"

"That would be great, Ian. If Kenzie is feeling up to it, she is more than welcome to come as well. This way she can meet Coach Pam and Coach Carol."

"I will see if she is up to it. Thank you."

"You are welcome, Ian"

The way she says his name at the end of her sentences makes Ian blush as he turns around for the exit door from the Sky Lounge. He makes his way past the elevator doors, because he knows he can take the emergency exit stairs down to his floor, one floor down, and will be able to access it with his key card.

Ian is moving so fast down the stairs that he is only landing on every other step. Once he lands on his floor, he swipes his access card, and the exit door flies open. As he exits the emergency stairwell into the twenty-second-floor hallway, the smile on his face just freezes, along with the rest of his body. That is because he notices Jax standing at his bedroom door, knocking.

Jax stops knocking on the door and just stares at Ian as he enters the hallway from the stairwell.

"Jax, what are you doing here?" Ian asks out of sheer surprise.

"I'm here because I thought you two were in some type of trouble," Jax answers back. "I went to Maria's room, but it was empty and now you are fine? What is going on, Ian?"

"To be honest, Jax, I can't explain any of this. Yes, Kenzie and I did not wait on you to come back to the school before going into Maria's room to look for clues on where she may have taken Connor and Brayden, but as soon as we got into her room, we both passed out. Then just a few minutes ago, I woke up in my bed in my room with Kenzie in Brayden's bed. Apparently, I carried her from Maria's room to here with no memory of it. I just confirmed this with another student, River Kate, who is in the Sky Lounge now preparing for a surprise party for Coach Carol. Kenzie is in my room, but will not answer the door because I told her not to answer it for anyone except me," Ian explains as much as he can to Jax. "Come in and see for yourself, and you can ask her about it."

Ian uses his room key and unlocks his bedroom door to open it so Jax can see that Kenzie is safe, which he does. Kenzie comes running and hugs Jax first, then Ian.

"What exactly is going on here? How are you two safe and not in Maria's room?" Jax asks.

Chapter 3

Where Are We?

"Brayden? Are you in here? I don't want to be alone. BRAYDEN!" Connor woke up in a nearly completely blacked out room, scared. "BRAYDEN!"

"Connor! Yes, I'm here with you. Thank you for waking me up. Who knows how long I would have slept, if you hadn't started yelling my name? How long have you been awake?" Brayden answers Connor's cries of panic, in a way to calm him down and hopefully make him feel useful instead of scared.

"I just woke up in this place, a few seconds ago, whatever this place is. What happened to us?"

"I'm not completely sure, but I think Maria set a trap for us. I don't think she was ever down in the lobby. She was in her room the entire time."

"Brayden, I may be young, but I can remember what she said in her room. I mean, what happened after that," Connor is not shy about how well he understands life.

"Sorry, but how am I supposed to know what happened? After you passed out from the sleeping spell Maria had placed on her room, I passed out too. Then you woke up screaming my name, waking me up. Now, we are both awake in this pitch-black room. Now you know what I know," Brayden rambles on like he's the child in the room.

"Thank you, Brayden. That is exactly what I was asking about."

"What are you talking about? I didn't tell you anything you didn't already know."

"Yes, you did. As you said, after Maria's sleeping spell knocked me out, it knocked you out, and we ended up here. I didn't know how we ended up here, but I do now."

"You got all of that from what I just told you?"

"Yes. If a sleeping spell made me fall asleep, also made you fall asleep while we were both in Maria's room, then obviously she has taken us somewhere away from the school. That is unless you can remember seeing, or barely seeing, this area in the school or in her room."

"Okay, Connor, you made your point. I was awake just a few seconds longer than you. That still doesn't help us figure out where we are, does it?"

"Relax, Brayden, we are going to be okay."

"And how do you know we are going to be okay? Do you know something I don't? Or are you just telling me that to make sure I'm calm?"

"Will you stop stressing out for a minute?" Connor says to Brayden, up front and cold. "I need a moment for my eyes to adjust to the dark, so at least I can get somewhat of a look around the room to see what we may be dealing with here."

"I know that! I was just about to suggest the same thing," Brayden snaps back at Connor, trying to gain control of the situation back from him.

Now that they are both awake and are finished going back and forth to see who is coming up with the best ideas, while each calming the other down at the same time, they begin to glance around to try and see if they can see some clue of their surroundings. Wherever they are being held, there are no sounds and there seems to be just a small crack in a door in the room, letting in light.

As Connor's eyes adjust to the darkness of the room, he begins to make out the small cell where he and Brayden are being held. He is more at ease once he notices that they are being held in the same cell together. He notices Brayden stumbling around, his arms stretched straight out, trying to feel his way around. This reminds Connor of a Zombie he has seen in old movies. This, in fact, makes Connor start laughing out loud.

"What are you laughing at?" Brayden asks.

"You!"

"Why are you laughing at me? You can't even see me. Can you?"

"Yes, I can see you. If you could see what I see, you would be laughing too."

"Well, since you can see, do you mind not making fun of me, and tell me about what else you see?"

"I'm sorry, Brayden. I am not making fun of you, you just happened to be the only thing I can see right now, and the way you were trying to feel your way around was funny to me. That's all. So, you know we are in some kind of room with bars all round it, and there are also two beds in it, if you can call that hard thing I woke up on a bed. I can see those things as well now."

"Is there a door?"

"It's really hard to tell right now, but I'm sure there is one, or how else how would they have been able to put us in here?"

"Fair point. Well, can you use your powers to bust open the door?"

"I won't know until I can find the door. Even then I would have to be able to see it and figure out how it's locked," Connor explains.

"Why do you have to see it? Can't you just look in a direction and use your power to push hard?"

"It's not that simple, Brayden. I have to be able to see what I am trying to move, or else I could end up moving the wrong thing."

"Like what? What could be the wrong thing right now? We are locked in a cage."

"Well, I might be young, but what would happen if I moved a wall that is holding up the floor above us by mistake?" Connor retorts to Brayden, needing no answer in reply. "Just give me a few minutes, please."

Connor takes a few more minutes to see if his eyes will adjust any clearer to the darkness, but they are as clear as they are going to get. He continues to move closer to one of the cell walls, with the hopes that he may be able to follow along it to a door. *If I can't use my eyes to see the room, then I may as well try using my other scenes to help,* Connor thinks to himself as he makes his move to the wall of bars that he can make out that is closest to him.

Just as Connor reaches the wall, he hears Brayden yell out, "Ouch!" This stops Connor from moving any closer and pulls his attention back over to Brayden to see what is happening to him.

"Brayden? Are you okay? What's going on?"

"Don't move and give me a second, please?"

Don't move? What is in here with us? Connor stands still with his mind running wild. "Well, what is it?"

"Don't touch the walls. They are electrified! I just went to lean on one, and the current almost knocked me out. Whatever you do, do not touch the bars making up the walls," Brayden insists to Connor, while trying to regain his bearings as he is lying on the cell floor.

Connor takes Brayden's advice and slowly makes his way over to him lying on the floor. "How long do you think we will have to be here before anyone shows up to tell us where we are?" Connor asks Brayden as he is taking a seat on the floor next to him.

"Not very long," comes an answer, but not from Brayden. "Not long at all."

***

Kayla looks directly into Mason's eyes and without missing a beat, her calmer body companion, answers for her, "Am I not allowed to even use the restroom without an escort?"

Mason does not answer right away. He continues to just stand and stare at her, unsure if he can trust that she has been where she says she has been, the restroom. He thinks a little silence may cause enough awkwardness for her that she may reveal something else. But neither Kayla, nor her body occupant, were going to break.

"Is there anything I can help you with, since you are in my room? Or were you just checking to see if I could follow instructions or not? And to be honest, I figured if you allowed me to walk to my room alone, and not send a guard to stand at my door, then I should be able to at least go to the restroom on my own. How was I supposed to know just how long you were going to be, and I had to use the restroom. So, tell me now if going to the restroom is going to be off limits, or may I be able to use it by myself from now on?"

"No, you are free to use the restroom whenever you need to, on your own. I'm sorry for overreacting. It's just that the meeting with Maria went longer than I anticipated, and she was more paranoid than her usual self," Mason apologizes to Kayla.

With Mason's apologetic words, Kayla takes that as her time to move out of the entrance of her bedroom door and walks over to her bed, passing within a foot of him. Her traveling companion is trying to convey to Mason that she has nothing to hide and is unafraid of being near him at the moment.

Any sign of fear from you right now, and he will know we are not telling him the truth, the companion thinks to Kayla, so she can understand why she has to be so close to Mason. Reaching her bed, she turns and takes a seat on the edge of it.

Now back in control of her own body, Kayla has some questions of her own for Mason. "So, what was your secret meeting with the crazy lady about?"

"Kayla, you know that I am not about to divulge any information that was discussed between Maria and myself. She was actually in the right by not wanting to have our conversation in front of you. Not that there is anything you can do to help, or hurt the outcome of it, but it will keep you from asking so many other questions. I hope I'm making myself clear about the subject." Mason explains to Kayla.

"I don't think you could be anymore clearer that you are being right now," Kayla replies.

"How about we discuss something we both have known, but I have not wanted to admit to," Mason tells Kayla.

Trying not to sound nervous, she asks, "Like what?"

"Like the fact that the traitor is gone. He was able to somehow find a way out of this building, and even away from this entire area without being seen. I have decided to stop looking for what can't be found and focus more on what, or who, helped make his escape possible in the first place. There is no way that he was able to achieve any of that on his own. He had to have had help."

"So, again, are you coming back to me for help, or to accuse me of something?"

"For your help, my Dear. My suspicions of you helping the traitor have been long past. But I think if we were to work together, instead of me forcing you to help, we may be able to get more accomplished. Don't you agree?"

"When do we get started?"

I will get back to my own body now and let you handle things from here. Just remember, you need to hide that ring we stole from Mason's office safe. Put it somewhere no one will find it, whenever he gives you a minute. Good luck. Kayla's travel companion bids her farewell and departs from her body.

"How about right now? Are you ready to get started?" Mason asks.

"I'm ready, except. Do you mind if I take a minute to change my clothes? I really don't feel this outfit is going to help me with interrogating people," Kayla asks in order to get some time alone to hide the ring.

"Yes, of course. I will wait outside your room for you. Come out when you are ready," Mason answers her as he turns and walks towards her bedroom door, exits while closing it behind him, never even turning back for a second glance.

As soon as her bedroom door shuts behind Mason, Kayla already has thought of the perfect place in her mind of where she is going to hide the ring. She remembers that when she was hitting the mirror, the one in her bedroom that she saw the vision of the store in, when she was looking for cameras in it that a small cap popped off the back that hides a screw hole in the wood. It is the perfect size for the ring to fit in, and she can just put the cap back over it to cover it up.

Kayla hops off the edge of her bed and makes her way over to her dresser. This way she can grab a change of clothes and hide the ring all at the same time, without wasting anymore time. She does not want to draw any undue suspicion from Mason by her taking too long to change. After the ring is placed in its hiding place with its cover over it, she grabs her change of clothes and heads over to her bed again to change.

Her dirty clothes are on the floor and her new ones are all buttoned. Now she is all set. She makes her way to her bedroom door, grabs the handle, gives it a twist and pulls it open. Standing in the hall, just as promised, is Mason. She exits her room, closes her door and walks up to him. "Ready?"

"Ready. Let's go," Mason replies.

***

As the three of them settle into a seat in Brayden and Ian's room, Jax, Kenzie, and Ian all just sit and stare at each other, not really knowing how to start a conversation about all that has happened.

"Okay, so who wants to start?" Jax asks the other two. "I got it. How about I start?

First, what part of me telling the two of you to stay out of Maria's room until I get back did you not understand? Do you think I was just telling you that because I like to hear myself talk?

Don't you dare, answer that Kenzie.

If I didn't have my own suspicions about Maria, like when I was leaving the school and made you aware of them, Kenzie, then I may be able to understand your motives. But I did tell you as I was leaving.

Second, again, why didn't you wait for me to arrive here? You both already knew I was on my way back. That was a careless move by the both of you. I won't even ask whose idea it was to ignore my orders in the first place, because I'm sure I already know the answer to that question. Kenzie.

Now, the third and final question, what do you mean both of you passed out as you entered into Maria's room? I opened her door and called out your names, and nothing happened to me. And if you were both passed out, how were you able to carry Kenzie all the way up here to your room, and yet have no memory of it? You were even able to confirm all of this from another student. And what does this student think you were doing with Kenzie? Does this student suspect anything odd about your encounter with them?

Now, I believe the two of you have quite a bit to explain," Jax finishes his reprimands to Ian and Kenzie. "I'll give you a few minutes to gather your thoughts, then we will discuss them all in detail. Understand?"

Chapter 4

Garrett?

Now, it is Ian and Kenzie's turn to explain things to Jax. While he has been getting something to drink from the mini fridge in Ian's room, the two of them have been speaking to each other telepathically, with Kenzie's help of course. Kenzie is upset that Jax suspects her as the one that disobeyed his orders, which is the truth, but hurts her all the same. Ian does not want to discuss how they got to his room with no memory of it, until he has time to investigate it more. So, they are at a standstill.

"One of you needs to start talking," Jax demands. But before either Ian or Kenzie could react, Ian's body starts speaking for him.

"Hello, Jax, Ian, and Kenzie. My name is Joseph, but my friends call me Garret, I have been the one who has been helping you Land Ian," he says while looking directly at Jax. "I helped you on the train, and I am also the one who carried Kenzie up here, with the use of Ian's body, of course. I know you all have plenty of questions for me, and I will answer what I can, but no more. There is too much at stake with this messed up timeline as it is, and I'm trying to help put it back on its correct path without altering it from that path. This is all I can say about my involvement, so if you don't mind, keep your questions limited only to specifics. Don't worry, I will answer Ian's questions as he thinks of them, only if they don't break my rules. Does everyone understand?" Garrett finishes explaining the rules with Ian's voice.

Jax and Kenzie are both still in complete shock that Ian is saying these things. Jax speaks first, "So, it was you that helped us on the train by telling Ian to sit in the passenger car and pretend to be asleep? How did you know that was a good, no, perfect time to do that and to have him tell me to do the same, in order for us to avoid Mason's men that were following us?"

"Yes, that was me, but I can't tell you any more than that about that incident. Let's just say there are some things I can confirm, but can't go into more detail about. I hope you understand."

"Okay, then, how can we trust you? How do we know you are actually trying to help us?"

"If I wanted to hurt you, any of you, I would have left Ian and Kenzie passed out in Maria's room, but I didn't. I made Ian's body carry Kenzie up to his room, where we are all standing now, didn't I?" Garrett clarifies with the group, including Ian, whose body he is still using to have this conversation with the three of them.

"You do have a point there," Kenzie interjects this time.

Jax gives Kenzie a stern look for having any reply to Ian's replacement.

"How did you know that Kenzie and you, I mean Ian, needed help in the first place?" Jax is not asking specific questions as instructed in the beginning by Garrett.

"Well, I can tell you I was otherwise engaged in another mission, when you," he says pointing at Kenzie, "vaguely appeared in front of me during my mission, causing the body I was using to freeze. I had no clue who you were at first, but I could tell you needed help. I had no choice but to leave the body I was using and follow you to Maria's room. Seeing Ian passed out on the floor, I knew something was wrong, so I quickly accessed his body. Once I was in his body, I had access to his memories, so I knew right away the two of you were in trouble," Garrett explains.

"You mean, I teleported to you?" Kenzie asks Garrett with confusion.

"Sort of. It was like you were there, but not all there. You were more of a shimmer of yourself, like a reflection in a pool of water."

"Jax, is it even possible for me to do that?" Kenzie questions.

"Well, since you were physically unable to teleport like you normally would, because you were under a sleep spell, your unconscious mind may have reached out for you. So, yes, I would say it is possible."

"But how would I be drawn to him? I don't even know him."

"Maybe he wasn't who you were drawn to, maybe it was the body he was using," Jax suggests. "Garrett, is it possible that any of us knows the person you were using during your mission?"

"I'm sorry, but I cannot answer that. That does not matter anyway. I'm curious though, about something that I went through once I was in Ian's body. There seems to be someone else already in his mind that was giving me a hard time with Ian's body controls. Would any of you know about that? I'm asking you as well Ian." Garrett questions.

"I'm sorry, but we cannot answer that. You understand I'm sure," Ian answers for the group with is body and voice. "Anyway, that does not matter now. You were able to get us here safely, so, thank you."

"You are welcome. Now, if that answers all your questions on how you got here, I must go. I need to get back to my body, so I can make sure my previous mission was a success," Garrett informs the group. "Then I will bid you all a farewell, but know I will still be helping." And with that, Ian is back in control of his own body. Garrett is gone.

"Now that explains a lot," Ian speaks for himself.

"It sure does," Kenzie replies to Ian, "that you have enough room in your head for at least three people."

"Ha, ha, ha, very funny Kenzie," Ian says as a rebuttal to Kenzie's comment.

"You two cut it out. Ian is right, that does explain a lot of things. He said that you teleported to him. Do you remember what you saw when you went to him?" Jax asks Kenzie.

"No, I didn't even know that I teleported while I was asleep until Garrett just told me. I wish we had Brayden here with us. He could walk through my dreams and see if there is anything there that would help, or at least see what happened, but he's not here. Neither is Connor," Kenzie reminds them of their current situation. "What are we going to do now, Jax?"

***

"Who said that?" Brayden asks in the dark.

"I am Maclaine, a guard that has been assigned to watch the two of you until you woke up. Then I was supposed to let Mason know."

"And how were you to let him know, Mason that is? You have not left the room, or light would have been let in. You also have not made any calls, or we would have heard you sooner. So, my guess is that he does not know that we are awake yet," Brayden confirms Maclaine's actions, still being unable to see him.

"You are correct. I have not informed Mason yet. I have been amused watching you walk around the cell like a zombie, then getting zapped by the cell wall. I did not want to ruin the entertainment I was watching. It was way too funny to interrupt," Maclaine replies with a laugh to Brayden. "But I'll tell Mason that you are both awake now."

Brayden and Connor sit silently on the floor of the cell they are in, hoping to hear how Maclaine intends on contacting Mason.

***

Kayla and Mason are in the control room when a guard walks up to them. "Excuse me, sir. I hate to bother you, but you wanted to know as soon as the guests were awake."

"Yes, I did. Thank you. Are they still in the dark?" Mason asks the guard.

"They are, just as you requested."

"Great. Thank you again for the fantastic news. You may go now," Mason says to the guard. "Kayla, would you like to meet our new guests?"

"Sure. Do the 'guests' have anything to do with you and Maria's meeting earlier?"

"You could say they do, in one way or another."

"Then what are we waiting for? Lead the way," Kayla says to Mason with enthusiasm.

The pair of them walk out of the control room and down the hall. Along their way, they pass both Kayla's bedroom and Mason's office, until they reach the elevators. These are the same ones that were supposed to be used to take the traitor down to the cells, which didn't turn out so well for the guards escorting him there. Upon arrival to the elevator foyer, Mason presses the 'down' call button.

While they wait for the elevator to arrive, Kayla can't help but wonder what she is getting herself into. She knows that if these guests have anything to do with Maria, then they could be people trying to help her or Ian. Either way, she does not want to jeopardize an encounter that could put any of them in harm's way. She needs to come up with an excuse, and fast, on why she can't go down with Mason right now. "Mason, do you mind if I meet you in a bit? I need to run to the ladies' room," Kayla asks Mason.

"Can't it wait? We are about to go down and meet the new guests."

"Mason, there are times when a woman needs to be excused, you don't ask questions, if you get my drift," Kayla tells Mason.

"Oh, I see. Yes please, take your time and go to the ladies' room. You and I can meet up once you are finished. Is that acceptable to you?"

"Yes, I am not exactly sure how long I may be. I'm going to need to change clothes as well. I will ask the guard for your location once I am ready to meet up with you."

"That will be fine," Mason says to Kayla as he steps into the elevator, which has arrived.

Kayla turns and begins her walk back towards her room. She knows if she wants her excuse to be believable, she will need to grab a change of clothes. Not to mention, she will need to take up a little more time, until she can figure out something to keep her from seeing the 'guests' Maria has brought. She reaches her bedroom door, gives the door knob a twist and pushes the door open. She steps in and closes the door behind her.

Now that she is in her room, she knows she only has a few minutes to grab her change of clothes and head to the restroom. Anything longer will look suspicious, if anyone is watching, and someone is always watching. Kayla makes her way to the dresser, pulls open the third drawer and grabs a shirt and another pair of jeans. She pushes the drawer closed and walks back to the bedroom door. Still unsure of what she is going to do, she opens her door and makes her way out into the hallway, closing her door behind her.

As she heads down the hall towards the bathroom, she continues to think of a way to avoid meeting Maria's 'guests,' or hoping that if she does have to meet them, neither of them will compromise the other. *What am I going to do?* she thinks to herself as she reaches the bathroom door. She turns the doorknob and pushes it open. While she is making her way into the bathroom, she is flooding her mind with more questions. *What if they are here and can help me, and I blow their cover? Or what if they blow my cover?* She is still thinking and shutting the door at the same time.

***

Switching from body to body takes quite a bit of energy from Garrett, but he knows it has to be done. He knows he had to complete his mission with Kayla, then explain the situation with Ian, Kenzie, and Jax, regardless of how much energy it took. Now, being back in the body he has been assigned for his school assignment, he knows he should rest, but he also knows there is no time.

The first thing he knows he has to do is to find Kayla. While he was in Ian's head, he saw something that he is not sure he was supposed to see. He also needs to find Mason to find out who these kidnapped kids are that he is holding as prisoners, on Maria's behalf. He is torn on what to do first, so he leaves his sleeping quarters in the barracks, and begins his way to Kayla's room. He is headed there first because that is where he last left Kayla, talking to Mason, right after their heist.

As he makes his way around the corner of the long hallway, he spots Kayla going into the restroom. Since he knows her location, he decides to stop and speak to her first. He can assume she is alone as there are no guards outside the door, and he knows she would not go into the restroom with someone else. He knows she values her private time.

Garrett rushes down to the bathroom door and gives it three knocks. He, of course, waits for a lady to answer a bathroom door.

"Who is it?" Kayla asks.

"Kayla, my name is Garrett. You do not know me by my name, but you do know who I am."

"How can I be expected to believe someone that is telling me that I know them, but not by their name? How else can I possibly know who you are?"

"By the fact that you and I stole a ring from Mason's office safe about an hour ago, except that I was using your body with you to complete that mission. I used your body to open the safe for you to reach in and grab the ring. Does any of this sound familiar?"

"You are HIM? The one that took over my body. Whose body do you have now?"

"I am actually in the body I have been assigned by my teacher for this project. I am about five feet ten inches tall, with brown eyes, but if you look hard enough into my eyes you can see a hint of green, and I have shiny dark brown hair. Some say this hair looks like a wig, but I don't understand the comment really. They also say it has a Clark Kent look to it from 'Superman.' Have you seen that person before? I was not assigned that period, so I don't know who that is. Will you please open the door?" Garrett begs Kayla.

Kayla opens the bathroom door and is shocked by the guard standing in front of her. Garrett was not at all what she was expecting. To be honest, she really didn't know, nor could think of, what Garrett looked like. The thought never crossed her mind. To her, he had no body, because he was using hers at the time. She is speechless and staring at him. *Superman indeed!*

"Hello, Kayla," Garrett says softly.

"Um, oh, hello body snatcher," Kayla replies, half joking. "I mean hello, Garrett."

"I'm sorry to bother you in your private time, but I don't have much time. I just left Ian's body, and while I was in it, I felt traces of someone else in his mind. Actually, not just one person, but two at one point. But one of them in particular was searching Ian's dreams and was focusing on anything that had to do with you. I am not sure if you know him, or if he knows you directly, but he does know about you and what you look like."

"I'm so confused right now! You, a guy that was in my body not long ago, are telling me that someone that was in Ian's mind knows me, or about me? What does that have to do with me right now?"

"I'm not one hundred percent sure just yet. If you can give me enough time to go down to the cells to find Mason so I can meet the new prisoners, I can tell you more. I just want to make sure you know I'm who I am. I'm going down now, so you can take longer to do whatever it is you are doing here instead of going down to the cells with Mason. This way I can see if either of them have been in Ian's mind. I will know them when I see them."

"Please do. Go down and see what you can find out, because I've been avoiding going down there for that exact same reason. Well, not the exact same, more like what if they know me, or if I know them, or they are here to help me and I blow their cover, type of situation."

"Okay. Stay here while I go down to see who they have kidnapped this time in the holding cells, and I'll get back with you one way or another," Garrett says to Kayla as he walks out of the bathroom, closing the door behind him.

Garrett makes his way down the hallway to the elevator foyer. His fatigue is catching up with him, so he knows he has to hurry. As soon as he presses the 'down' call button, the elevator doors automatically open. *Great, I didn't have to wait too long,* he thinks to himself.

Garrett steps into the elevator and presses the button for the basement. The elevator doors close and it begins to make a slow, but quiet descent down. Once the elevator makes it to its destination, the basement, the doors open to a pitch-black room. *This is going to be harder than I thought.*

Chapter 5

In the Dark?

"Who's that coming down here? Is that you, Kayla?" Mason asks as the elevator door closes behind Garrett.

"No, sir. It's me, Garrett. I heard we had new prisoners, so I wanted to come to check on them. I was informed that you were already down here, so I thought now would be the perfect time to check them out."

"Well, it's good you are here then. Where have you been anyway?"

"Sorry, I've been tied up with some other business, looking for the traitor. Now that that has been called off, I can focus more on your needs here. If that's okay with you, sir?"

"Yes, that's fine. Thank you for coming down here. We may need some other guards to help get these two in line."

"Yes, sir. So, what are we dealing with here? Why are the lights off in this room?"

"They are off for some added protection for us. We know one of them can move things with his mind, while the other is able to 'Dream Walk.' With them in the dark, they are unable to see us to use their powers against us, not that they could anyway. I have spells in place preventing any of their powers from being used while they are in our custody."

"If you have spells protecting this place, then why are you keeping the lights off? How can you see them?"

"Here, put these on. We are using night vision glasses to see them, so they can't see us," Mason says to Garrett while handing him a pair of glasses for him to use.

Garrett takes the glasses that are offered to him and puts them on. It takes him a minute to get a view of the entire room, before looking at the 'guests.' Then as he sees them for the first time, he freezes. *That's him. That's the one who has been in Ian's mind and knows Kayla.* Garrett thinks to himself with shock.

"So, what do you think, Garrett? Do you think they will be hard to put in line?" Mason asks.

"Not at all, sir. I'm pretty sure I can have them conforming to our way in no time, without any help. So, I don't think any more guards are going to be needed," Garrett replies to Mason. He is hoping he will get the opportunity to be alone with them, so he can talk to them about Kayla, and not blow her cover. "I think leaving the lights off is also best for a bit of extra protection."

"I couldn't agree more. Even though Kayla has not made it down here yet, I see no need for her to come down here now. I am going to go back up and find her and leave you two here to see what you can get from them," Mason instructs Garrett and Maclaine.

"The two of us?" Garrett asks Mason.

"Yes, you and Maclaine. He is the guard that has been assigned to them since they arrived. I believe he could be of some help to you. Do you have a problem working with someone else?" Mason questions Garrett.

"No, sir. I just did not know who I was going to be working with. Sounds like Maclaine and I should be able to get these guests in line fairly quickly, working as a team," Garrett replies, knowing that this is not the actual situation he was hoping for.

"Good. That's what I was expecting to hear," Mason relates to both of them. "Now, I will leave you two here to get acquainted a bit before you begin working on those two."

Mason turns around in the dark and walks towards the elevators. He is still wearing his night vision glasses. Once he reaches his destination and presses the call button for the elevator, he removes the glasses. He knows that wearing those glasses when the elevator doors open with the light shining inside could cause him to go blind. He has actually seen one of his guards do this by accident. The man spent over three months in the infirmary. He never did gain his eyesight back.

Mason thought about that guard as he waited for the elevator to reach the basement. Just about that time, the elevator doors made a loud 'ding,' then the doors opened up. Mason steps in and presses the button with the 'L' on it, for Lobby. He knows that is the floor that Kayla is on and then he is gone from the basement.

"Well, Maclaine, how long have you been down here watching them?" Garrett tries to get as much information as he can from the other guard.

"Let's see. I've been down here since they got here," Maclaine snaps back at Garrett.

Garrett knows now that this is going to be one long mission. He also knows that Maclaine is not going to be helpful at all. He will have to come up with another plan of action, if he wants to get any time alone with the guests. He has to think of something quick, because he is not sure how much longer he is going to be able to continue without getting some rest.

I've got it! Garrett thinks to himself.

Garrett tells Maclaine that he is going to go and grab something from his room, something that will help gain the two prisoners' cooperation. He then begins walking over to the elevators. As soon as he reaches the elevators, he quickly presses the call button, while asking Maclaine to join him at his location, because he has found something!

"What do you need me to do with whatever it is that you have found?" Maclaine mouths off to Garrett.

Knowing the elevator could arrive at any time and the doors open, he makes another plea to Maclaine. "I think this is something of Mason's. But if you don't care about it, then I'll throw it away. If he starts looking for it, I'll make sure he knows it was your idea to toss it," Garrett replies with no problem with the thought of going through with his words.

"No, wait! I'm almost there," Maclaine replies back to Garrett's bluff as he comes stumbling around the corner, where Garrett is waiting. "Now what is it that you found?"

Just as Maclaine is finishing his question, the elevator door opens up, filling the area the two of them are in with a bright light. "I'm sorry about that, Maclaine. Are you okay? Are you able to see, or do I need to escort you to the infirmary? I totally forgot about the elevator, and I had already removed my night vision glasses," Garrett is trying to make it all look like it was just an accident.

"I'm fine, Garrett. It's so nice to see how much you care about my wellbeing and all, but you can stop the act you are putting on. My eyes were closed as soon as I made it around the corner. Why do you think I was stumbling? Now, do you want to tell me why you are trying to have alone time with these kids down here?" Maclaine comes back at Garrett with direct questions.

"I'm not completely sure I understand what you mean. It was just an accident," Garrett says in return to Maclaine's allegations, trying to keep his cover intact.

"Let's make a deal. You tell me who you are working for and what you are doing down here, and I will do the same for you. And no more lies, because I had already figured you were not one of Mason's real guards when you said you could interrogate them alone."

"Let's say that what you are suggesting is true, but if we had that kind of conversation you are requesting, who is to say this is not a trap? And who is to say someone is not listening to us now?" Garrett questions Maclaine.

Brayden chimes in, "You both know that WE are listening, and can hear you, right? We are just in a cell with bars for walls, so your voices carry right through into our cell for us to hear."

"I wasn't talking about you two. I was talking about Mason, or someone in the control room," Garrett responds.

"You don't have to worry about them hearing or seeing us right now. There are four cameras down here, but they only have video. None of them have audio, so no sound. Now as far as the video goes, they cannot see us in the dark, so it's best if we leave the lights off for now. So, ready to talk?"

"All right, you win. To be clear, there will be a lot of things I cannot tell you. Not because I don't want to, but because I can't. The reason is because I am not from your world, or time. If I say too much, then the timeline won't be fixed and could be damaged more than it already is. I do not work for anyone, but I am helping Kayla, Ian, Jax, and Brayden, just in different ways, to make sure that this timeline is repaired. Something happened recently, so the future changed, and Kayla went missing. But before I found her here, I had to help Ian, Jax, and Brayden make it to school safely. This is done by me taking over someone's body," Garrett is letting it all out.

"That was you, on the train, which talked to Ian through my body?" Brayden speaks out again.

"Yes, Brayden, that was me. Sorry, but I wanted you all to be able to rest, so you could be prepared for what happened at the Houston Train Station with Mason and his men."

"Can I ask you a question?" Without waiting for a reply from Garrett, Brayden asks anyway, "Why did you apologize to Ian for contacting him?"

"Because, if things go wrong and I can't fix the timeline, then I find out that it was because I have been contacting any of you, at the time it was Ian, I wanted him to know how sorry I was for causing such torment and damage in his life," Garrett replies to Brayden.

"Now, does that answer your questions about me?" Garrett asks Maclaine.

"Some, but it will do for now. Guess you would like to know about me now?" Maclaine says to the group.

"Well, a deal is a deal," Garrett confirms that HE is at least ready.

"Fine. I am actually here on Maria's orders, and before anyone freaks outs, she is not on Mason's side," Maclaine starts out with his explanation of who he is and who he is working for, as his part of the deal.

"You mean to tell us that you are working for the person who put a sleep spell on us, kidnapped us, and brought us here, wherever here is? Here to be locked up in this electrified cage. And this is supposed to make us trust you?" Brayden is fuming with the questions now.

"Yes, but if you will allow me to explain, you will see that Maria is not who you think she is," Maclaine answers.

***

"I'm not exactly sure, just yet, what we are going to do, Kenzie," Jax replies.

"There has to be someone you can contact. Or someone who can lead us to a good starting point to get answers on 'Garrett,'" Ian says to Jax.

"I do have someone I need to speak to about this. I didn't get to finish my conversation with them earlier, because I was pulled back here. But what will you do while I am out?" Jax says to Kenzie and Ian.

"I can assure you that we will not be snooping or spying on anyone this time. I can promise that the two of us will be waiting for you to return before we do anything," Jax can hear the conviction in Ian's voice and believes his words to be true.

"Then on that note, I will go ahead and go back out to where I was before all this happened. There are still quite a few questions I need to get answers to. I will be back as soon as I can," Jax reassures Kenzie and Ian as he makes his way to Ian's bedroom door and exits.

"Well, Ian, what do you want to do now?" Kenzie asks.

"I know you might think this is weird, but I am actually thinking of taking a nap for a bit," Ian replies to Kenzie.

"You want to do what? Are you kidding me? You just had your body invaded by, we don't actually know what, because we were sleeping. Now you want to take a nap?" Kenzie is not joking about her questions.

"I know you are upset, and I can even understand why, but I need to see if I can talk to Junior. He is the original person that first broke into my dreams and showed me memories of the past and future. I know it sounds silly, but I believe he may be able to answer some questions for us, now that he is back," Ian explains to Kenzie.

"Fine, but I am going to stay here with you in your room, just in case sometime happens or goes wrong," Kenzie demands.

"Thank you," Ian replies to Kenzie as he makes his way back over to his bed. Once he reaches his bed, Ian lies down on the bed and gets comfortable. This is a nap he really wants to take.

***

Jax pulls up, again, to the place where he grew up. The place where he was taught about the Believers and how the rest of his life would be lived based on their beliefs. This was where he grew up to become the Believer he is today. After this meeting today with Chancellor Billie June, he may feel a bit different, or that is what he is afraid could happen.

The last time he felt this nervous was at his graduation. Luckily, he made it back just as the sun is rising, and even though he is extremely tired, he wants to speak to the Chancellor first thing this morning. He is ready to finish their conversation about Maria, Junior, and even what Ian can do to correct everything with the timeline.

Jax parks his car and makes his way into the front entry of the glamour placed over the mansion he just left yesterday. Walking into the grand entry, he is greeted, again, by the same young lady as yesterday.

"Welcome back, Jax. Will you be needing a room to stay in tonight?" She asks Jax this time instead of insisting.

"Not this time. I do, however, need to speak to the Chancellor as soon as possible. Is there any way I can speak with her now?" Jax replies to her offer.

"Yes, she is actually expecting you now. If you would follow me, please," the young lady says to Jax.

Jax follows his escort over and across to the hallway to the Chancellor's office. They make their way down the hallway towards her office door. As they approach, the door begins to open, as if she truly is expecting him.

Once they reach the open door, his escort turns and begins to make her exit back down the long hallway, away from Jax and the Chancellor's office. As Jax is alone, he makes his way into the office. Then upon entry, he closes the office door behind him.

Now that he is in Billie June's office, he calls out for her, "Chancellor? Are you here?"

"Yes, Jax. I am here. Everything was okay when you got back to the school?" Chancellor Billie June asks.

"That all depends on how you answer my questions. It seems we still have much to discuss," Jax confesses to the Chancellor.

"More than you even know, Jax. More than you could possibly know," are the Chancellor's words to Jax.

***

Kayla is still waiting in the bathroom for Garrett to return with any information he is able to gather about the new 'guests' of Mason's, when a knock on the bathroom door startles her. *I hope this is Garrett,* she hopes to herself. "Who is it?"

"It's me, Mason. Please, open the door."

"Okay, I just need another minute. Sorry I've taken so long, and I'm pretty sure you don't want to hear the details," Kayla replies to Mason's request.

"No, take all the time you need. I do not need any explanation. I am just here to tell you that you are not needed down in the basement. Things are being handled as we speak," Mason tells Kayla, really wanting to avoid any explanation or details of why she is still in the bathroom.

What does he mean it's being taken care of, and I don't have to go down there now? Kayla is now worried about Garrett. "Is everything okay with your new guests?"

"Yes. I have two of my very loyal guards that are going to be taking care of the interrogation for now. This means we have some free time," Mason tells Kayla.

"Oh, that's good, I guess. I was really looking forward to trying to break someone's spirit today," Kayla replies, hoping to sound convincing enough for Mason to actually believe she means it.

"I'm sure you were, but now you don't have to worry about that. Is there something else you would like to do today instead?"

"To be honest, I have never had a free day here, unless I was locked in my room," Kayla said to Mason as she opens the bathroom door. "What is there to do around here, when you are not interrogating prisoners or looking for traitors that is?"

"You know what? That is a very good question. This is the first time that I have had some free time also," Mason admits to Kayla. "I guess we'll just have to play it by ear. What do you say about that?"

"Well, no plan sounds like the best plan we can have for today," Kayla replies. "I'm ready if you are."

"Then let the day of no plans begin."

Chapter 6

The Favor?

Kenzie patiently waits on Brayden's bed as Ian takes his nap that he has to have. The last thing she wants to do right now is to sit and wait while her little brother, Connor, is still out there somewhere with Maria. *I hope he is okay. I'm glad that he is at least with Brayden*, Kenzie thinks to herself to help keep herself calm about her brother's absence.

As Kenzie does what she can do to remain calm, Ian has fallen asleep. He has been asleep for about an hour. He is getting the nap that he has been wanting. Kenzie has not worried about Ian's nap, as he has been sleeping calmly. He has not been talking in his sleep or tossing and turning. He has just been sleeping.

***

Ian is walking along the cliffs on the Big Island of Hawaii, Kona. The cliffs he is walking along are part of South Point Park to be exact. As he is walking, he is looking over the edge, watching the water. The blue and clear as crystal liquid, washes up against the side of the Island, then rushes back out into the ocean. Once the water recedes back out, Ian is able to see other cliffs just below him. Some of these cliffs have puddles in the rocks, while others lead into caves that go through the side of the cliffs. Then the waves come back with a roar, covering the cliffs again. The cycle repeats itself.

Ian looks up just in time to spot a Great White shark out in the water. South Point Park is not only the most southern point of the Islands of Hawaii, but also for the United States. More Great Whites and other large marine animals can be seen from South Point Park than from any other place in Hawaii.

Hearing someone scream, Ian looks to his right to see if there was someone hurt, or if he could help. But what he is witnessing is what is called "jumping South Point," referring to people brave enough to cliff jump off and take a forty-foot fall into the ocean below. "There is no way I would ever do that," Ian says out loud in his dream only.

Ian turns his attention back to the waters ahead of him. Water that looks as if it will never end. Then he notices the sun setting. He can't help but be mesmerized by the beauty of the sun hitting the water with no ending. Ian turns around and realizes that from South Point Park, you can watch the sun rise and set from one spot, and the sun will be over the ocean the entire time, for the whole day.

South Point Park is one of the most beautiful places Ian has ever seen, yet he knows he has never been there, or to any part of Hawaii. This is exactly what he is hoping for during his nap. He wants to speak to Junior and now he knows he is there in his dreams. Junior is showing him memories of one of his relatives. *I wish this were my memory, but I now know its Junior's.*

How did you know it was me? What gave me away?

How about we start with some of my *questions first? Remember the last time I saw you, which just so happened to have been the first and only time I met you, you vanished right in front of me. You also told me that your mother is Kayla, my best friend, who is still erased from history, or this timeline. Speaking of that, how are you here, if Kayla is still erased from history? If you are back, does that mean we actually do find her and restore what's been done?*

Junior begins, *Ian, the future is a very uncertain and fragile thing. I may be here now, meaning things are going in the right direction, but the slightest change in your plan, and I could vanish again. The future is all up to you. Only you can choose your right path that you want. It may not be the best path for you, but sometimes in life you have to make a choice. It may not always be the right one for you, but it may be the right one from someone else. That is why you and your powers, with the Time Keeper, are so valuable to Mason. He wants to have a life he was not meant to have, and he will destroy every other life to get what he wants. This is what makes him so dangerous. This is why he can never get his wish.*

Junior takes a moment and shows Ian another memory. This one is of someone he does not know, but he does know the room he is in. They are in the room from his dreams. The one with the four-post bed, fit for a king, a fireplace large enough to walk in, and red wallpaper with a crest on it. The gentleman gets up from the chair where he is sitting, which is on a handmade rug covering the polished hardwood floors, and walks over to the large double wooden doors. He grabs the door handle on one of the doors, and pulls it open, walks through it, closing it behind him, and makes his way down the hall to a magnificent grand staircase.

Ian follows the man, he assumes is a relative, down the stairs, only one floor down. Once they reach the main level, the man starts his walk across the room. Slightly to the right side, he turns down a smaller hallway. At the end of this hallway is just one door. Ian follows his family member down the hall to the door. As they approach it, the door opens on its own before they could even reach it.

Ian follows the man through the now open door and spots someone that he does know, Maria. Maria is here with an older woman, who seems to be in charge. They both greet Clint, as we walk through the door. Apparently, Clint is a teacher at the school for the more advanced special students. He is in his late thirties with brown hair and eyes and tan skin. Clint greets them both back, "Hello, Maria and Chancellor Billie June. I'm sorry we are meeting under these circumstances."

"We are as well, and thank you for coming on such short notice. What has happened really affects us all," Maria says to Clint.

"I couldn't agree more."

"So, what are we going to do now? Who is going to be able to go undercover as Head of the Believers and infiltrate Mason's group? This is the closest we have ever been to getting in," Maria asks, while holding a photo of a couple in it. Ian watches Maria turn the photo and notices some writing on the back of it, but can't make it out.

"I think it should be you, Maria. I know this goes against everything you believe in as a person, but I have faith you will be able to pull this type of mission off," Chancellor Billie June chimes in.

Ian can't believe what he is seeing, or hearing. *Could Maria be helping us? But she has done so many terrible things,* Ian thinks to Junior.

Yes, Ian, people are not always how others see them. Many people live double lives. Some live them because it is the only way they can be themselves and happy, while others do it because it's just their job. Maria is doing her job, even if she

doesn't like it, but she also knows it has to be done, Junior
thinks back to Ian.

Who are those people in the photo, and what do they
have to do with any of this?

What I am about to tell you, you have to promise you
will never repeat it. Not to anyone, ever. Do you promise?

Yes, I promise.

Those people in that photo that Maria is holding are
Connor and Kenzie's parents. When word got out that their
mother was going to be the next Head of the Believers, Mason
approached her and tried to get her to align with him and work
against the Believers to get the Time Keeper to him. Once she
refused, he followed her home. But before she had time to tell
anyone what Mason had asked her to do, he brought Mr. and
Mrs. Green to that timeline to break into their home and wipe
both parents' memories. Memories of them ever meeting,
knowing each other, having children, or ever knowing anything
about this world. Then he took Connor and Kenzie and gave
them to the Greens to raise as their own, for the work they had
just done for him.

That's messed up. How can someone do that?

I told you Mason is very dangerous, like most desperate
people are.

So, Maria took Kenzie's mother's place, and went
undercover to try and stop Mason from getting the Time Keeper.
That's why she took Brayden and Connor. She needs them to
help her with part of her mission, but not to blow her cover.

Yes, now you know more than I should have told you,
so you are never to reveal anything I have shown or told you
tonight. This information is for you only. Do you understand?
My life depends on it.

I can promise you that I will never repeat any of what
I have seen or heard here tonight from you. I want Kayla back
as much as you do. Well, you may need her back more than I
do, but you know what I mean. Can I ask you a question? Who
is your father?

To be honest, my mother never really talks much about him. He is not in my timeline.

I'm sorry I asked. That was a bit too personal.

No, it's okay. I just know that he is a very good man, at least that's what my mom tells me. Now, Ian, I hate to go, but I am not fully up to my full strength yet. You can still sleep, but I have to leave you for the night.

Trust me, I understand that. Why do you think I'm taking this nap? I needed rest as well, but I also wanted to make sure Jax and Kenzie were right, and that you really were back. I'm glad you are back, and I will do whatever I have to make sure you never leave again.

Thank you, Ian. I can see why you were my mom's best friend growing up. You really do care about her. That is the last thing Junior says to Ian, before he releases him from the memory he was showing him. Once Junior is gone, and the memory fades, Ian is back to just dreaming.

Ian sleeps for another two hours before waking up. When he wakes up, Kenzie is sitting right beside him, looking him directly in the eyes.

"So, did you enjoy your nap? Was it everything you hoped it would be?" Kenzie asks Ian.

"It was just a nap. I'm not sure what you were expecting, but I do feel better now that I have been able to sleep, on my own and alone in my head," Ian replies. "Have you been watching me sleep this entire time?"

"Yes, I have. I have been watching you sleep, because you have a bad habit of going to sleep and not waking up for a few days or talking to people in your sleep. I had to stay awake to make sure you WOKE up."

"Fair enough. I'm sorry I have put you and the others through so much. I know I can't control my sleep, or dreams, so thank you for taking such good care of me."

"So, you got nothing? You only slept? I don't understand the point of the nap."

"It was to get some rest," is all Ian tells Kenzie about his nap. He leaves out his entire interaction with Junior and everything that was told to him about Kenzie and Connor's parents and Maria. But he couldn't help but to feel sad for everything she and Connor have been through, and didn't even know the half of what their parents went through, and still are going through. He smiles at Kenzie to reassure her that everything is fine, and his nap was just a nap. He can only hope that Kenzie won't slip into his mind to read his thoughts at some point in the future and find those memories. If that ever happens, he knows that their friendship would be over, considering he just lied to her. The last thing he wants is to lose Kenzie's trust. She is one of his only allies right now.

"Fine, if that is the story you want to stick with."

"It's not a story, it's the truth. Do you want to search my mind just to prove that I am telling you the truth?" Ian asks Kenzie, praying she does not call his bluff. The last thing he wants is for Kenzie to find out the actual truth about his nap and the fact that he just lied to her.

"No way do I want to sift around through your boring dreams. There's no telling what boys dream about, and I am not ready to find out what you boys dream about now. Not at my age, not ever," Kenzie replies.

As Ian lets out a breath of relief. Kenzie lets out a big yawn of her own. "Hey, why don't you grab some rest yourself? It's still early and now that I have rested, you can let me watch over you while you get some sleep. Let me take care of you for once," Ian tells Kenzie.

"I'm not really tired. Plus, I'm too worried about Connor and Brayden. I know Brayden will never let anything happen to Connor, but what if they are not together? What if that evil Maria has them separated? Poor Connor. He will be all alone and scared. How am I supposed to sleep with all of this on my mind?"

"First, remember that Connor may be your little brother, but he can move things with his mind. That means that if anyone were to try and hurt him, he will just throw them against the floor, wall, or ceiling without breaking a sweat. Second, I don't think Maria will separate them. I think she took them because she needs them, or their powers together, so she will want to keep them both calm and comfortable. In other words, I don't think you have to worry about them, but you do because that's what big sisters are supposed to do. It does not make you a bad sister, if you take some time for yourself, instead of worrying about Connor. I think he will want you to be rested and at your full strength when we do find them. You will be no good to them or yourself if you are falling asleep during the rescue mission," Ian soothes Kenzie's mind and his own in the process.

"I am a little bit tired. Are you sure things will be okay? And if they are not and something happens, you will wake me up as quickly as possible, won't you?"

"You have my word. Now, why don't you go over to Brayden's bed and lie down and get a nap of your own."

With these words from Ian, Kenzie turns, walks over to Brayden's empty bed, crawls inside the covers and falls asleep in seconds. Now it's her time for a nap.

While Kenzie takes her nap, Ian moves about the room, trying to find anything to do, so he does not think of his conversation he had with Junior during his nap. He is afraid that just thinking about his time with Junior, while Kenzie sleeps, she may accidentally access his thoughts, and that is not something he is going to let happen. He made a promise to Junior and just lied to Kenzie, so he will be letting two people down if she finds out, on purpose or even by accident.

Ian checks around his dresser again, looking for the ring Kayla gave, or gives him, even though he knows Maria has it. After searching around his dresser, he decides to check inside each drawer, and by doing so, he takes out all his clothes in each drawer and tosses them onto his bed. Not finding that special ring from Kayla, he folds his clothes and places them back into each of the five drawers of his dresser. He knew he wouldn't find the ring, but he knows he has to keep his mind active and thinking of anything other than his nap. After all the clothes are folded nicely and back in their respective drawers, Ian makes up his bed, cleans the small sitting area, all while not disturbing Kenzie as she gets her much needed rest. He continues to clean his room for however long Kenzie needs to sleep. He is not going to wake her or let her peak into his thoughts.

Kenzie gets a good four hours of deep sleep, then wakes up to Ian cleaning the bathroom, from what she thinks maybe the second or third time he has cleaned it since she went to sleep. She can tell he has been doing a lot of cleaning by the looks of his room. The only place that looks like it has not been dusted, waxed, or washed, is Brayden's bed. Kenzie suspects that is because that is where she was sleeping, and Ian didn't want to disturb her rest.

"Kenzie, you're awake. Did I disturb you and wake you up? I'm sorry if I did. I really was trying to be extremely quiet so that I wouldn't disturb you," Ian apologizes to Kenzie.

"No, you didn't wake me. You were very quiet, so thank you. I slept just fine, until I had this strange feeling that woke me. I'm not sure if it is just in my dream or if it is real, but it was enough to wake me," Kenzie replies.

Chapter 7

Camryn?

"You see, I'm a former student of Maria's. When Maria chose to take on this mission, she wanted to have someone on the inside that she knows and can trust. She reached out to me and asked if I would do this with her," Maclaine explains to Garrett, Connor, and Brayden down in the cells, while still in the pitch dark.

"And why would you do something that is this dangerous for Maria?" Garrett asks, for his own information.

"Maria has always been a mentor to me. Whenever there was something I didn't think I could do, she would push me and make me prove to myself that I am the only person that can ever hold myself back from doing anything. I don't know if I would have made it through school without her 'tough love.' This woman sugarcoats nothing. She tells it like it is, which honestly works for some people, like me, but it definitely does not work for everyone. It works for me, so when she asked me to do this with her, there was no question in my mind about whether or not if I would help her. It was only a question of when we go?"

"I will agree with you that she says what she wants, no matter what, or who she offends," Connor replies out. "She still scares me!"

"Oh, don't get me wrong. Her bite is as bad as her bark. She just expects the best out of everyone. She sees more about people than they may see about themselves," Maclaine clarifies to Connor about Maria.

"Then what does she want with us exactly?" Brayden asks of Maclaine.

"She wants you to help her with the timeline. Since you are both here now, she wants you to tell Mason you are both now willing to join his group and help them find out information from other people, Kayla especially. Mason does not trust her," Maclaine replies to Brayden.

"So, Maria is not going to let us go anytime soon? So, I won't get to see my sister? Kenzie is going to have to worry the entire time that we are here. That's not fair," Connor tells Maclaine.

"I know it's not fair, and so as soon as we get a chance, we will get word to Jax, Ian, and Kenzie that you are both okay. We want them to be preparing and not worrying about you just as much as you don't want them to worry. I promise, Connor," Maclaine tries to ease Connor's stress.

"Now that we have all of that worked out, when is all of this, or any of this, supposed to happen? We need to make sure we are just as ready," Garrett tells Maclaine.

"I am not completely sure about when Mason is wanting to start the interrogations. And he did not give me a timeframe to get these two, Connor and Brayden, ready," Maclaine says, while pointing at the two in the cell. "But if we take too long, he will remove us and put someone else down here to work on them. You know as well as I do that if we get pulled off and away from them without some plan, we will most likely never get the opportunity to come up with one later," Maclaine tells Garrett. "We need to come up with something, even if it is just a basic plan for now. We have to make sure we have something in place, just in case Mason does relieve us from duty, you know, if we don't move fast enough for him."

"You are right, half a plan is better than having no plan at all, for now. You said that Mason is going to use Brayden and Connor to get information from people. Do you know who he is going to use them on?" Garrett asks for more details from Maclaine.

"I know he is planning on using Brayden to dream walk people to get information, but he didn't say which people he plans on invading their privacy. The only person I know for sure that he is expecting Brayden to dream walk is Kayla. He trusts her the least, no matter how much she does to prove to him her loyalty, he still feels it is not genuine. He can tell when someone is not telling him the truth, or even just a partial truth."

"Good to know. Are you getting all of this, Brayden?" Garrett asks.

"Yes, I can hear Maclaine talk just as well as you can. If I have to dream walk Kayla, I have to be prepared to be able to fool Mason into thinking she knows nothing about nothing. But what if she doesn't know anything? Remember, she has been wiped from history and that includes this timeline, which, in turn, includes Ian and everything else regarding him, or us," Brayden inquires.

"We can only hope that she does not know anything. We do not know exactly what questions Mason will be asking you about Kayla's dreams, or thoughts, after you dream walk her. His thoughts maybe totally different than ours, so his questions could be different as well. You will have to be prepared to lie to Mason and make him believe you are telling him the truth. One small mess up, and he could throw you right back down here along with Garrett and myself," Maclaine emphasizes on how important Brayden's performance to Mason has to be after his dream walk of Kayla, regardless of the questions asked.

"He's right, Brayden. The only thing we know for sure is Mason's endgame, which is to get the Time Keeper. We do not know how he expects to achieve that goal or what methods he will use, much less what questions could be in his twisted mind," Garrett also speculates to Brayden.

"We know what he wants Brayden for, but what does he want with me?" Connor asks from the darkness.

"Let's hope I never have to tell you, and it never gets that far Connor. Let's hope we can do this before he needs, or wants to use you. One thing is for sure, we will need you to get us out of here when the time comes," Maclaine tries to avoid telling him what it is exactly Mason wants Connor for, if it gets down to it.

***

"And what more do I need to know, Chancellor? I know we didn't get to finish our conversation yesterday, and you have some things to tell me about Kayla and the ring, Ian repairing the timeline, and Maria's involvement," Jax questions Chancellor Billie June.

"You are correct, Jax. We have many things to discuss. Now, I will be able to tell you some things in part, but not fully. The reason is not because I don't want to, but because I don't want to put predetermined thoughts in your head. I want you to be able to make a choice when the time comes down to it. Do you understand?" Chancellor asks.

"In a way. But in another way, it sounds like you know more that you are letting on, and not just the part about you taking the Time Keeper during Sebastian and Grayson's fright. And that you don't want anyone to know about it, whatever it is that you know. To me that is suspect, because what you did as a little girl was the right thing to do, and you told me about it. So, you not telling me about something else, makes me think you did some things that were not the right thing to do," Jax remarks to the Chancellor's opening statement.

"You could be correct in your assumption, Jax, because none of us are perfect. We all make decisions every day, some are good, while others, we may not enjoy so much later in life. But that's why they call it life and also why I want you to be able to make your own decisions, or choices, on certain things that we may talk about, but I won't finish explaining."

"Now, I understand the logic behind you not wanting to tell me everything."

"Good, then we can begin with where we left off. Now, where were we?"

"You said you have an idea about how Junior is now back in the future timeline, now that Kayla has touched the ring."

"Awe, yes. Now I remember, the future is always changing from this point on. And by this point on, I mean by every moment of your life, until that moment passes and becomes the past. Understand?"

"Yes, you have not lost me yet. I am a history teacher, you know," Jax replies with a little humor.

"Well, what I am about to tell you is a part of history you have never been taught. This is a part of my history from when I was that little girl. The one who went against the rules of our people, the Believers. The girl who stole the Time Keeper, to create a ring, a ring for Camryn, Jacob Helen's first-born child."

"By all means, do tell."

"As Camryn grew older, her mother, Jennifer, did exactly what her husband asked of her and gave the right he made to their daughter, Camryn. Now, what you don't know is that this ring has been given down for generations, by the females of the Widdill family bloodline. They carried on this tradition for many generations, until as luck would have it, the ring came up missing. This, of course, was not because of any of my doings. As you remember, I was already removed from watching Sebastian, and no one knew about the Widdill family ring, except me."

"If the ring came up missing, then how has it ended up here in this timeline, and Kayla is not here to get it?"

"Now that is an enigma in itself, isn't it? How could her ring be here, and she not be here? Well, that is the problem with time travel, things don't always work out the way someone plans for them," the Chancellor expresses with a hint of sadness in her undertone. One could think that she is reliving her own mistakes as a young Believer, never getting a chance to put the Time Keeper back in its rightful place before time ran out.

"In other words, in order for her to ever get the ring, the ring must first appear in our timeline. Even if the ring starts out from the future, unless we fail and she does not receive the ring during our timeline, then the cycle will be broken? But then if she does get the ring, won't she be creating a cycle in history? She will have it and have to come back at some point in her life, and try to break the cycle again. If that's the case, how many times have we already done this?" Jax asks in the simplest way he possibly can.

"When time is irrelevant, then the number of times someone has repeated something in history doesn't really matter, does it? But the meaning of the word 'insanity' is doing the exact same thing, over and over again, expecting a different outcome. I can tell you that if this is not the first time this has happened, you, or we, are not insane," Chancellor Billie June taunts Jax's mind.

"If we are not insane, and we are not caught in some type of history loop, then what would you call us? Why wouldn't we be called insane?"

"It's very simple, Jax. Who said anything about this being repeated in the first place? Also, if it has been repeated, do you honestly think we would allow the same things to be tried, over and over again, in the exact same way?"

"I didn't think of it that way. I'm sure, as the Chancellor of the Believers, if this has been repeated, then you would have made sure that measures were taken to ensure we do not make the same mistakes that we have possibly already made in the past," Jax confesses.

"I will not admit to anything, but I won't deny anything either. Let's say you may not be the only one who may have to change a few things now and again," Chancellor says with a smile.

"Now that we have cleared up that repeating of time issues, what actually happened to the Widdill ring? How does it just come up missing?" Jax brings their conversation back to the loss of the ring.

"Jax, this part of their story could lose you. I will be brief about it, because we could talk in circles for years about this one incident."

"That bad? Or just one of those things you can't completely tell me?"

"Both so here goes. No one is for certain when, or how, the Widdill Family ring originally came up missing. But a grown Kayla, who goes by her middle name Alexis, actually finds the ring in the exact same antique bookstore where Ian's parents found the Time Keeper.

"At the time, Alexis is looking for something to give to her unborn child she is carrying. As she goes by that store, the ring always stands out to her, and it has for many years. So, she decides to get it for her son, Junior. She wants to have something to pass down to her child, like her best friend Ian's family does, with the Time Keeper."

"So, you are telling me that Junior is Kayla's son, from the future? The same Junior in Ian's mind right now? The same one that Ian said vanished right in front of him after showing him memories of his relatives?"

"I'm not sure exactly what you are talking about, Jax. What do you mean when you say that Ian hears voices in his head? Is that how you would describe it? Ian's hearing voices?"

"Sort of. Let's just say that not only has Ian been hearing Junior, but Kenzie has also been in contact with him as well. Kenzie and Brayden were both kicked out of Ian's mind during a failed attempt to help him access the Time Keeper, by someone, who by the way, she describes him as someone who calls themselves Junior. Ian first encountered him before he and I ever met. Ian said that this person, Junior, showed him memories, some of the past and some he believes to be of the future. One of the memories he was shown involves the room upstairs that you put me in. The one with the red wallpaper on the walls, with the large fireplace, the room on the second floor. Would you know of any of Ian's relatives ever staying in that very room many years ago?"

"I can think of one of Ian's relatives that did stay in that room, except at that time, the Time Keeper was missing. With the Time Keeper missing and Clint not having it, EVER, there is no way he could have stored a memory of that room in the Time Keeper."

"Well, if 'Clint' didn't store the memory of the room in the Time Keeper, who did? Better yet, why did they store a memory of that room in the first place?"

"First of all, we don't actually know if we are speaking about the same person, 'Junior.' The person Ian, Kenzie, and Brayden have been dealing with may say his name is Junior, but that does not mean that he's the same Junior that is Kayla's son. We may be dealing with someone completely new here, Jax. And you say that Ian has been in contact with this person in his head from before Kayla wiped herself from history?"

"Yes. Ian said that he was having dreams of these places and me, which I spoke to Ian in one of those dreams, telling him those were memories, not dreams and I would explain it to him more when the time was right. Later, Ian was informed by 'Junior' that he was the one that was showing him those memories. He said he came back from the future to try and change it and needed Ian to do it. But by the time 'Junior' was able to reveal himself to Ian and actually speak to him, person to person in his mind, admitting all of this, 'Junior' began to vanish as soon as Kayla being wiped from history caught up to his timeline. As he was vanishing, he confessed that his mother's name was Kayla, then he was gone."

"Then how is he back now? Something does not sound right about this 'Junior.' How can he have access to one of Ian's relative's memories in the first place?

There is no relation between Kayla's son and Ian, so he would never have access to the Time Keeper, yet alone have the memories of Clint, who never put any memories in the Time Keeper."

"But aren't you saying that Kayla is a descendant of Camryn Widdill? If that is the truth, then isn't it possible that 'Junior' can access the Time Keeper? If his family ring was made with a piece from the Time Keeper, to bond the ring as part of the Hele family bloodline? Also, wouldn't that also mean that Ian and Kayla are related, since her family bloodline is also from the same one as Sebastian's?"

"Again, those are the questions that I cannot confirm, nor deny, but you are a very smart man, Jax. I'm sure it won't take you long to figure out the answers to those questions on your own."

"Then let me ask you a question you may be able to answer. Who is Kayla's son, Junior's, father? If you can answer this one question, then I will have what I need to be able to make a good assumption of my previous questions?"

"You are correct, Jax, that is a question I can answer, but to be honest, I don't think that will be something that you can handle knowing at this time," Chancellor Billie June leaves those words with Jax, as she turns and begins to walk out of her office.

"Chancellor, wait! You still have not talked to me about Maria," Jax reminds Chancellor Billie June.

"You are right, but that conversation will have to wait for another time. You and I both have some important things that need to be done right now. I will tell you this though, help Maria when she asks for it. Don't ask questions, just do what she asks," are the Chancellor's final closing remarks as she walks out of her office, shutting the door behind her, leaving Jax alone in her office.

Chapter 8

A Free Day?

Having a full day with Mason is not exactly Kayla's idea of a free day. As their day continues, all she can think about is the last time she and her mother were supposed to go shopping. On that day, while she was getting ready for the day, she noticed the small watch attached to the end of her necklace that Alexis had given her, along with the ring to give to Ian, started working for the first time. Not only was it working, but the watch hands were also moving in the wrong direction, they were moving counterclockwise. She also remembers that was the moment that she was erased from history!

Thinking about that day is making it hard for Kayla to enjoy any type of fun for her free day today. All she can think about is her mother and father. She is wondering how they are doing, or if they are even together, since she was wiped from history. She doesn't know if they even meet in a timeline without her.

"What's wrong, Kayla?" Mason inquires.

"Oh, it's nothing," Kayla responds.

"Are you sure? You don't seem to be having very much of a good time out here at the shooting range."

"I must say, going to the shooting range is a first for me, but really it is okay. It's just something else on my mind right now. It's not you, or the shooting range. I promise."

"I'm sorry that I don't have many places I can take you to, but we have to keep this place a secret. I wish I could take you out of here for our free day, but this is how it has to be. We can't afford to let anyone learn of our location or what we are actually doing. You understand that don't you?"

"Yes, I do, but what I'm thinking about doesn't matter, because it never happened. Now, in this timeline, my parents never had me. Therefore, they don't even miss me. But I get to live my life remembering them and missing them. You may choose not to believe Alexis, but I do. I know I had parents that don't even know I exist anymore, so they don't even get to feel the pain I feel every day! Can you imagine how I must feel? No, you can't! I can though! I know I have parents, and I know I wiped myself from history for some reason. I may not know exactly why I did, but I did it just the same. That means my parents have no memories of me, all because I made a choice to erase myself. Why would I, or anyone for that matter, do something like this to themselves, or their parents? And not even just to them but to every friend they ever made?"

"I can't answer that question for you, Kayla. It's partly because I don't believe Alexis, and another reason is because you don't seem like anyone who would erase themselves from history. What is it that you do in the future that is so bad that you think you would have to go back in time and do such a thing to change what you did? Or in reality, have someone else erase you for you? Which if you ask me is a very selfish act, and you don't seem like a selfish person, to me anyway. You could not be more opposite then myself, which I am very selfish, more than anything in the world. You have more goodness in you than anyone I can think of. Don't ever think of yourself as a bad person, or even a selfish one, because no matter what you do here with me, for me, you will be doing it for the greater good. That alone makes you a good person in my eyes. And trust me when I say I know a lot of bad people, so I can tell the good from the bad."

"I'm glad you feel that way, because I don't. I can't think of any reason I would want to make my parents forget having me, or even being together. Can you?"

"I can, actually. My mother died when I was very young, leaving my father to raise me by himself. My father was not the most reliable parent a child could ask for. There were days he would not even come home; therefore, I didn't even have food to eat. Then, as I grew older, there were days he would come home drunk and would blame me for his crappy life and my mother's death. Then he would beat me until he was too tired to continue. This went on until I decided to run away at sixteen."

"I'm very sorry. That sounds terrible."

"Well as they say, 'What doesn't kill you makes you stronger,' or 'Behind every cloud is a silver lining.' While I was living on the streets, I met a group of people. The group that took me off the streets. They were called the Believers. It was being part of this group where I learned about the 'Time Keeper' and the powers it holds. With access to their libraries and books, I was able to discover that I am a descendent of Grayson Zimmerman, who was the best friend of

Sebastian Helen. I was not only told about the secrets of the Time Keeper, but how it had been missing for many years. That is until Ian received it on his seventeenth birthday. Once I learned the Time Keeper had been found, I left the Believers. I then was given a mission in life, and that is to get the Time Keeper from Ian, by any means possible."

"So, you're telling me you turned your back on the very people who took you in when you had no place to go? Just like that, they meant nothing to you anymore. How could you turn your back on the people that took you in off the streets, cared for you, and taught you so much, just like that? So easily?"

"That coming from the girl who claims she came back from the future and erased herself from history to stop something that she causes to happen. Let me ask you the exact same question that you just asked me. What is your answer?"

"That is not a fair question to ask. I don't know why my future-self came back and erased us from history. But you do know why you betrayed the Believers, the group that took you in and helped you when you needed it the most in your life. Therefore, you can answer the question, while you know I can't. Not yet!"

"You are correct. I can answer that question, but remember I think you can too. I think you just use an excuse that is not even possible, to cover your reasons to have run away," Mason tells Kayla with a definitive ending to the subject.

About that same time, Maria is brought down to the shooting range and interrupts Mason and Kayla's free day.

"Mason, can I speak to you for a moment? In private preferably," Maria asks.

"Now? You can't wait until later to talk about whatever you have on your mind this evening?" Mason replies.

"No, this is very important. This is something we need to discuss now. Something has happened that I can't explain, and it is a bit disturbing," Maria tells Mason.

"Kayla? I hate to ask, but do you mind going to another part of the compound, so Maria and I can discuss her crisis?"

"You mean, do I mind going to my room?"

"No, I mean, you can go anywhere you want to in this place, but you have to stay within the compound. I just need to have time for a short conversation with Maria, if you don't mind."

"Well, thank you for part of a free day. I know I already ruined it earlier. Maybe we can try again another time?" Kayla relays to Mason.

"Maybe we can."

"Then I will leave you two alone," Kayla said to Maria and Mason as she makes her way out of the shooting range for her destination unknown.

As Kayla makes her way out of the range, Mason looks to Maria and asks, "So what is so important that you have to interrupt my free day with Kayla? And this better be good, because I have been doing my best to gain her trust. I don't need you coming in and disturbing all I have done so far, for something unnecessary," Mason conveys to Maria just how he truly feels about this situation.

"Let's just say that when I got back to the school, there was no one in my room. It was empty. There is no way that someone could have made it past my traps. They would have had to have had help, whoever they were. I know that someone was in my room, but when I got there, they were gone. Now, I need to know how someone could have gotten into my room, overridden my defense spells, and removed whoever was in my room in the first place. Not to mention, find out who it was that was actually in my room," Maria expresses to Mason.

"And you are absolutely sure that someone has invaded your room while you were here?"

"Yes! I know for a fact that my room has been broken into. I have no idea how they could have been able to escape, but they were unable to disarm my protection spells, and I know they were activated. I was notified once they entered my room and they triggered the spells."

"So, you are telling me that you have decided to interrupt the only free day that Kayla and I have ever had to tell me that no one was in your room? Oh, and let's not forget, you don't even know who broke into your room," Mason sarcastically retorts back at Maria. "Basically, you came here to disrupt our day, because yours did not go as you hoped it would, correct?

Now that you have made our free day all about you, why don't you go and check on your guests and see if Garrett and Maclaine have been able to achieve a better day than you have?"

***

"You mean that if Brayden can't get the information Mason wants, then he may use me to use my powers to force them, in a much harsher way, to talk?" Connor asks again about why Mason needs him here.

"Now, why would you want to go there, Connor? We don't know for sure what Mason wants with your powers. But they could be used for something other than hurting someone. He does not have to have you here for you to torture people for information Mason could need to draw Kenzie here. Did you ever think of that? Remember, Maria and Mason just found out about you having any powers, Connor. This means that Maria taking you has nothing to do with your powers at all, but more with who you are," Brayden explains to Connor with hopes of bringing his thoughts back from the dark side.

"I'm asking because of what Maclaine said earlier. He said, 'Let's hope I never have to tell you.' That pretty much sums up what he thinks I'm here for."

"I'm sorry I said those things to you, Connor. Honestly, I want you to be prepared for anything Mason may throw at you. Remember, he will be expecting you to cooperate, and he will be able to tell if you are telling the truth or not.

So, the only things you should be thinking of right now are of all the things Mason may ask you, and be prepared to answer him as honestly as you can, and make him feel that you are telling him the truth. Not just what he wants to hear, but the actual truth. If either of you can't pass his test, then Garrett and I both are gone, and someone else will be put in charge of breaking you two into actually following Mason's orders.

Now, do you all understand just how important this next meeting with Mason is going to be?" Maclaine gives the group a rude awakening.

"Maclaine is right. We need to stay on point here. We have no clue about what questions Mason will ask you, but one slip up and we are all toast," Garrett chimes in.

It was at that moment when the sound of the elevator doors opening catches all of their attention.

"Hey, whoever this is coming in now, don't say anything about me, but I am going to sneak back up to my room for a minute. As soon as they come this way, I am going to get back on the elevator and go back up, but I'll be back before Mason gets here. I promise," Garrett tell Brayden, Connor, and Maclaine as he makes his slip along the side of the wall beside the open elevator, waiting for the new visitor to walk past. Once they walk by, he makes his way into the elevator and is gone.

***

Kayla leaves Maria and Mason there on the grounds of the shooting range, but she is still unsure of her true destination. This is the first time she has been told she could go anywhere she wants on the compound. The thought of going anywhere on the compound intrigues her. She has never ventured off course before from where Mason has told her to go, unless it was the time her body was taken over by an intrusive guest, forcing her to break into Mason's office to steal something from his safe. Now, she is on her own and can go anywhere she wants to go. Too bad she can't think of any place in here, Mason's compound, that she wants to go, or anything she wants to see.

With no desirable places to go, Kayla wanders aimlessly down the compound's halls. She walks past Mason's office, then she passes her room, and on down the hall until she reaches the entrance sitting area. The same area where she and Mason had been sitting, waiting for Maria to arrive with her mystery guests, Brayden and Connor. Kayla takes a moment to try and remember as much about them as she can, for that brief time she was able to see them as they were being carried in Mason's guards. Finding it hard to focus on either of them, as they were being carried in, she gives up on the impossible and is at least okay with knowing their names.

Kayla decides to move on from the front entrance area and move on to another area she has not been to before. As she has only been in the sitting area once, she never really took notice of much of her surroundings in the room, so she begins to look around more carefully. This is when she notices a mysterious hallway near the edge of the sitting area room. She didn't notice it before as she was more focused on avoiding conversation with Mason, and then there was Maria's arrival. Once Maria had arrived, Kayla's focus was on Brayden and Connor, as they were carried by the guards and into the downstairs holding cells. Now that Kayla has noticed the hallway, she thinks of whether or not to venture down the unknown hallway. After about ten seconds of thought, her mind is made up. She WILL take a peek down the hall and see what lurks at the end of it. Now that she is able to go anywhere on the compound, why not?

Kayla makes her stance up off the chair she has been occupying to begin her way over to her new destination, the new hallway. As she makes her first move towards the untraveled hall, she stumbles over a small box that is sitting on the floor next to the same chair Maria sat in after she arrived. Unsure of what she has just stumbled over, she bends down and picks up the tiny ring size box. After a short scan of the package, Kayla decides not to open it at the moment, as she is more interested in the newly found hallway and its final destination. She places the box in her pocket for the time being, and continues on her path.

Kayla makes her way to the beginning of this new hallway, and upon her arrival, she immediately notices that there is only one doorway in it which is all the way at the end. At first, Kayla is a bit skeptical about going down the hall and seeing if the door is unlocked. After a quick minute of debating with herself, she chooses to keep going. *"I have come this far, why would I turn back now?"* She says to herself, then proceeds onward down the hallway towards the door.

As she progresses from the beginning of the long, mysterious hallway passing nothing but blank, bare, grey walls, she is reminded of an airport terminal as people walk down the tube onto the plane just without the cheesy vacation posters hanging everywhere. For a quick moment, Kayla stops in the middle of the hall, because she thinks she hears something. Unsure of what the noise could be, she waits for it to sound again, while hugging up against the hall's wall. She waits and waits, but there is not another sound. Now that she believes the coast is clear and that the sound is more than likely her imagination, she continues her walk in the direction of the lonely door at the end of the hall.

Kayla is moving at a burglar's pace, just in case it is not her mind playing tricks on her, and she really did hear a noise. As she reaches the door, she moves even slower, until she has her ear pressed up against the door itself, ever so gently. She takes a deep breath and just listens. Kayla is listening for anything out of the ordinary, or even ordinary. She is listening for noises, voices, chairs moving, or anything that could have made the sound she heard a few minutes ago from the other side of the unusually placed door. To her surprise, she hears nothing, just a calm silence.

With a silent room on the other side of the door, Kayla decides to take her journey a step farther. She reaches down and places her hand, softly, on the door handle, gripping it slowly and tight. With her tight grip on the door handle she gives it a very easy, slow, slight turn, and again is surprised feeling the door beginning to open. Kayla gives herself a quick smile of accomplishment and does not realize that she is not the only person turning the door handle. As Kayla begins to quietly push the door inward, the door is pulled open in a fast motion from inside the room.

With a jolt and a slight scream, Kayla begins to fall forward. Just as shocked as Kayla, so is the person coming out of the room, who also gives a small screech of fear. Instinctively, the person reaches forward quick enough to catch Kayla before she has a chance to fall completely into him.

"I'm so sorry. I really wasn't trying to sneak around. I have been given free time, and I saw this hallway, and my curiosity got the better of me. Please, don't tell Mason what I've done," Kayla explains to the man holding her.

"Kayla? I can't believe it's really you," the man holding her replies.

"Yes, but how do you know my name? Oh, I'm sure everyone here knows my name by now, 'Poor Kayla, Mason's guest, slash, prisoner.' Well, I'm sorry but I don't remember ever meeting you before, there are so many people here."

"No, that's not what I mean. And you don't really feel that is what people here think about you, or say about you, do you?"

"Yes that is how I feel. How else should I feel? I am not here because I want to be, like the rest of you. I have been brought here and left here with Mason. I can't leave. Not that I have any place to go. I don't even exist anymore, not that you would understand," Kayla finishes her story softly. "And by the way, who are you?"

"Sorry. We have actually met before, but not in the traditional way. Hi, my name is Garrett."

Chapter 9

Portal?

"What were you dreaming about that woke you up?" Ian asks Kenzie. "What kind of feeling disturbed your deep sleep, if you are sure it was not the noise that I was making while cleaning?"

"I promise it has nothing to do with your OCD cleaning mode. Oh, and WOW, what an amazing job cleaning you have done," Kenzie reassures Ian. I am not sure what I was dreaming, but I have, or had, the strongest feeling that Connor was scared. It only lasted a second, but it just felt so real."

"Were you able to see anything around him, or see him? Or did you hear him or any other sounds? Tell me exactly what you felt that made you wake up from your nap. This could be a way for us to find them, if it were not a dream," Ian presses Kenzie for more details about her experience while she was asleep. He knows a thing or two about things coming to him during his sleep. *Maybe she has been given the same thing*, Ian ponders.

"This was not something I have felt or done before. That's why I'm sure it's just my imagination, mixed with some wishful thinking to gain my connection with Connor back. You know when I have a mental connection with someone, I only see their thoughts, not through their eyes. Again, the feeling only lasted a few seconds really. All I could feel was fear."

"Fear? Are you sure it was Connor, real or not? Are you sure it couldn't have been Kayla, or even Jax?"

"Yes, I'm sure. The fear I felt came from Connor, real or not. But like I have already told you, I'm sure it was just my mind playing tricks on me. I'm sure it's just that I miss him so much and am the one feeling fear for him, not knowing where he is or how he is doing. Do you mind if we change the subject now, please? If we keep talking about Connor, I may just start crying," Kenzie pleads with Ian.

"Okay, how about... Do you feel rested at least?"

"Actually, I do. With everything that has been going on, I honestly felt like I could have slept for a month."

"Do you know that there is an actual sleeping disorder called Kleine-Levin Syndrome? Some people call KLS 'Sleeping Beauty Syndrome.' KLS is a very rare condition, mostly in males, that causes them to have periods where they may sleep for an extended amount of time in a day, or even two days. In some cases, it can even last for months or years. During these long term long-term episodes, sometimes the affected person may only get up to eat and use the restroom, then head back to sleep. Many of the people with KLS at an adult age end up having to move home with family members to take care of them. Remember how I said it was rare? Well, for an adult male to get it is even rarer, like one in a million chance. An adult male can start showing signs in his early forties to fifties. Being this rare, it still happens. Knowing all of this, would you want to sleep for a month?" Ian fills Kenzie in on a little medical knowledge he remembers from his health teacher, Bobby Young.

"Well, thank you, Ian, you have now turned a wonderful thought into a learning lesson. I know we may be in a school, but health is not one of my classes right now. By the way, we are not in a class right now, we are in your room. But now I need to know, is there a cure for this 'KLS?' And why is it only in males?" Kenzie replies, now with some curiosity.

"I thought you didn't want to have class today?"

"I don't really, but now I want to know what the people with KLS are up against in life."

"Fair point. Well, there is no actual cure for KLS, nor is there any specific reason, that anyone knows, why it affects males more. Good news is that most young boys do grow out of it before becoming an adult. Those who can't take different medications to help them with their symptoms. Now, adults are a little bit trickier. Adults have to take several medications of sorts, to see what may work for them, but the meds are not 100% effective for everyone. There are many of the adults with KLS that either control it, or it passes and goes back to being dormant, sometimes after about four years. This is also not a guarantee, but it is hope for them," Ian compassionately explains to Kenzie.

"I see what you just did there. You are pretty smooth, Ian. I'm sure you already know this about you. You should be proud."

"I have no clue what you are talking about or what you think I've done. I am just telling you something you didn't know about a sleeping disorder."

"Well, you did leave one thing out."

"What is that?"

"What happens to the adults who take the medications, and they don't work, or the ones that don't get through KLS? What becomes of them?" Kenzie sadly wants to know their fate in life.

"Remember when I said some people with KLS have to move home with family to take care of them? Those are the ones who have to move home. They sometimes can have episodes lasting up to a year. Therefore, they are unable to work or even take care of themselves, so their family members become their caregivers. They still keep the hope that their KLS will become dormant like the others, but it doesn't for everyone. It's a hard disorder to be told you have, not knowing if you will be one of the ones who will be able to pass through it, or be stuck with it, putting a burden on your family for the rest of your life," Ian speaks to Kenzie as if he knows more about KLS than he's letting on to her.

"Thank you for telling me. Now I know why you left that part out. I am thankful for the lesson, even the one you claim you didn't give. You have taught me that hope is a very powerful tool, an emotion to have, just like the last thing found in Pandora's Box. After the evil was released into the world, the only thing left in the bottom of the box was hope. Zeus willed it to remain in the box until Pandora could put the evils back, as he knew she could, because she was neither evil nor malicious. How am I doing so far?" Kenzie is trying to school Ian as a favor.

"Wow! You got all of that from my explanation of KLS? And is that true about Pandora's Box only having hope in it after she opened it?"

"Yes, it's true, or as true as Greek Mythology is to some people. You mean you really didn't know about Pandora's Box?" Kenzie is very happy with herself at this moment, knowing she has been able to teach Ian something he didn't already know. Before

Kenzie could continue to enjoy her victory, Ian's cell phone begins to ring.

"Hello," Ian answers his phone to see who is calling him. Ian sits for a moment with the phone to his ear, not saying a word, just listening. Then the silence is broken. "You want me to go where and do what? You have got to be kidding? What you are asking is forbidden in the school. I think I have another solution that will work better for us and not get us expelled," Ian finishes the rest of the conversation in a soft tone, too soft for Kenzie to hear.

Once Ian finishes talking with the person on the other end of the phone, he hangs it up quickly and turns his attention over to Kenzie.

"So, who was that, and what was that all about? It sure sounded like someone is wanting you, or both of us, to break some rules. I can only think of one person who breaks the rules around here, and I'm sure Maria is not calling you. So, out with it, who was it?" Kenzie inquiries from Ian.

"I will fill you in on our way. Right now, we need to change into some more streetwise, because we are going to be leaving the school for a little bit. You up for a field trip?"

"Getting out of the school with no adults to watch us, well that sounds awesome. I'll be ready in about five minutes," Kenzie boasts with satisfaction.

"Then we will leave in five minutes," Ian confirms with Kenzie, so they can prepare for their adventure out into Houston.

***

Jax stands there, alone in the Chancellor's office, still trying to piece together all the information Billie June has given him on this trip.

Like information about how Junior could be here for now, but be gone again, just like that. And just how did a relative of Ian's store a memory of the room at the Believers' Mansion, when Clint was not even in possession of the Time Keeper at any point in his life? Then you have the possibilities of 'Junior' not being the same Junior, which is Kayla's son from the future. But to top it all off, Kayla could be a descendant of Camryn Widdill, the long-lost bloodline of the Helen family. So much to take in at once, now realizing he needs to get back to the school, NOW.

Jax collects his thoughts and controls his mind from going any further astray, pulls his cell phone from his pocket and dials Ian's phone number. The phone begins to ring, and in only a matter of seconds, Ian answers.

"Ian? I need you to listen very closely to what I am about to tell you. I need you to go up to the roof and open a portal for me, here where I am, because I need to get back there as soon as possible," Jax instructs Ian.

Ian is not very happy about having to break the rules of the school, using his powers at the school, so he comes up with an alternative solution for the portal.

There is a pretty long pause on Jax's end of the phone, while he listens to Ian's protest, at first, and then to his solution to their problem. This is the only part of the conversation Kenzie was able to hear on her end.

"How about Kenzie and I go to the Houston Waterwall? I can open the portal there and not break any rules of the school, plus I will have a much larger area of water I can use," Ian tells Jax in a soft tone, on his end of the phone.

Jax remains silent while he listens as Ian finishes changing the plans Jax has carefully laid out. After giving Ian's new plan some thought, Jax decides it's not a bad idea at all. As a matter of fact, it's actually a better plan since no one from the school will be the wiser of what is going on in the first place.

"Your plan sounds like a very solid plan, Ian. I believe we should do this your way, since you know your powers better than anyone. Maybe you should be the person to pick the location. So, how long is it going to take you two to get to the Houston Waterwall? And you don't want to use a school car. You will want to take any other type of local transportation," Jax suggests.

"Right now, during this time of day, it should only take us roughly around thirty minutes to make it out to Waterwall Park. I will have Kenzie reach out to you once we are getting close, so you can get into position. For now, you should be looking for a place I can use as a portal where you are. Once you find a place, get to learn it very well. You will have to describe it in great detail to Kenzie, so she can tell me, so I can get a picture in my head to find you. This will be the only way I can create a portal where you are, since I don't know where you are and Kenzie and I have never been there, I assume. Are you getting all of this?"

"Yes, Ian, I am. I can actually retain more information than you may think," Jax quips back to Ian.

"Then I guess we will be calling for a ride, and you will need to start looking for a place to walk through. We will call for you shortly," Ian tells Jax and hangs up the phone before Jax could even reply.

Jax looks down at the phone in his hand, then just puts it in his pocket. "I can't believe Ian just hung up on me. Well, maybe I can," Jax admits out loud to himself. Then he begins his search for a place where Ian can make the portal.

***

"It's time for us to go. It's been five minutes. Are you ready to go?" Ian asks Kenzie.

"What if I told you that I have been ready for three minutes already? Would you think I was ready to go? Because I am so ready to get out of here. I am just waiting on you," Kenzie replies to Ian with a big smile.

Ian and Kenzie make their way out of Ian and Brayden's room, and into the hallway of the twenty-third floor of the school. Once the door is shut and locked, they head towards the elevators and press the 'down' call button and wait. Both of them are hoping for no surprises during this elevator ride. As they stand in front of the elevator doors, waiting to see which of the three will make it up to them first, Ian is using his cell phone to request a ride with one of the ride-share apps.

"Our ride will be here in ten minutes," Ian tells Kenzie as he puts his phone back into his pocket. "These elevators better pick up their pace."

"How far is the place where we are going?"

"It should only take us about thirty minutes to get there, but you never know with this Houston traffic. From what I have heard, if you leave a minute or two earlier than you planned, you may arrive at your destination way earlier than expected. Then on the other hand, if you leave one or two minutes after your planned time, you may end up at the same destination an hour late. The roads here are so confusing to me. Being from Brooklyn, I'm used to taking the subway and buses, which are reliable. But here, you get on a highway that has no stoplights on it, yet you could sit in the same place for ten minutes or more. Then the next thing you know, you are moving, and the traffic is gone, just like that, with nothing to show why you were stopped in the first place," Ian finishes as the middle elevator doors open.

"Finally, our ride to the lobby is here, and it's empty," Kenzie announces to Ian.

The pair steps into the empty elevator, while Ian presses the button for the Lobby. The doors shut and the elevator begins its descent to the lobby of the school. So far, the elevator has made no stops on any other floor to pick up anyone, which is a good thing for them both. They are already passing the tenth floor and still no stops. Just when they think they are going to make it all the way down to the lobby without any unplanned stops, the elevator stops on the eighth floor. Ian and Kenzie look at each other. Neither of them have to say, or think, a word to each other to know what the other is thinking. All they can do is take a deep breath and wait for the doors to open and see who gets on the elevator with them.

The moment has come, and the elevator doors begin to open. As the doors open, Ian and Kenzie look at each other, they suddenly relax when they see other students getting on the elevator. But Ian is surprised again by River Kate being one of those students.

"Hello, Ian, Kenzie. It's great to see you are feeling better now. Do you know what made you sick?" River Kate is speaking to Kenzie, while looking briefly at Ian.

What do I tell her, Ian? Kenzie thinks to Ian.

Tell her it was just a stomach bug, but it's already passed, Ian thinks back to Kenzie.

"Oh, it was just a twenty-four-hour stomach thing, but it's gone now. Thanks for asking," Kenzie replies to River Kate.

"Well, that's good to hear. You did not look very well at all when Ian was carrying you earlier when

I ran into you two in the elevator. It's good to see you walking on your own now, and since you are walking on your own now, will I see you and Ian at my party tonight?" River Kate expresses to Kenzie.

"Thank you for the invitation, but Ian and I are headed to the mall now. It really did look worse than it was, whatever it was I had. It must have just been a twenty four hour bug. I was just asleep when Ian was carrying me to my room."

"Well, who says there are no true gentleman left in the world today? Just when I thought all honorable men were gone from this time, you show up," River Kate is now addressing only Ian.

"I was just doing what any friend would do for another sick friend. It is no big deal, really," Ian replies to River Kate shyly.

Before River Kate could say anything else, and with the entire elevator already listening to their conversation, the elevator doors open. They have reached the lobby and the others have already begun to exit the elevator like a herd of sheep, one at a time, all except Ian and Kenzie. River Kate looks back and says, "I hope we can finish our talk another time soon, Ian."

"I have a feeling we will, very soon," Ian replies. He watches as River Kate walks away, smiling.

And just what was all of that flirting about? Is there something I don't know? Kenzie thinks to Ian.

It's nothing. I swear. You are more than welcome to go through my thoughts if you don't believe me, Ian thinks back to Kenzie as he leads the way out of the elevator.

As they are walking towards the exit of the school, Ian takes out his phone, takes a quick glance at it and put is back in his pocket.

"Who was it? River Kate?" Kenzie is mocking Ian.

"No, it's our ride. They are here. So, if we don't want to miss it, we will want to get outside now, before he leaves," Ian replies.

Chapter 10

Puzzle Pieces?

After hearing the elevator doors open, Garrett makes his escape from the basement. Brayden and Connor quickly remove their night vision goggles and hide them under their sleeping mats on the cots provided for them. The last thing they want right now is to be caught wearing the goggles, because that would give away that Garrett and Maclaine are helping them.

"Maria, may I ask what brings you down here?" Maclaine asks. Since he is still wearing his night vision goggles, he can see that Maria is the one who has gotten off the elevator, the one that Garrett has used to sneak out of the basement to run to his room for something he needs.

"Mason suggested we come down here to check on your progress with these two. But at the last minute, Mason said he had something he needed to take care of first and for me to go ahead and come down here alone and see for myself. This could not have been the best thing he has ever suggested. Now, have you filled Brayden and Connor in on everything?" Maria asks Maclaine.

"Yes, I have been able to inform them on some, but we have not finished with the debriefing. They both know that I am working with you and both of us are against Mason. I have also informed them that Mason will be coming down to interrogate them, and their answers have to be either the truth, or a very believable lie, even to themselves, or Mason will know it's a lie."

"That's good. I hope when I leave here and return to Mason, I can tell him that they are both cooperating, and he will take my word about it. If he does take my word for it, it will keep him from coming down for their questioning. But it's still best to be prepared.

Connor, Brayden, I want you both to know how sorry I am if I scared either one of you. This is the only way for Mason to believe me, and trust that my loyalties are with him and his cause. Connor, to be honest, you were a surprise to us all. No one knew about your powers, but they will come in handy, but not in any way Mason expects them. Brayden, you were actually the target of my trap that was in my room. You have a very important task to do, and I know you can do it. I caution you though, you cannot, under any circumstances, reveal the truth about what you will learn, and Mason must believe you."

"What is it that Mason is going to have me do exactly? And why would I have to lie about what I might learn?" Brayden asks Maria for more details about his role in all of this.

"For the record, everything Ian has told you about Kayla has been the truth. She did come back from the future, and she did erase herself from this timeline, but not completely. Everything about her has been erased. Everyone who previously knew her, now has no memory of her, except Ian. No one is exactly sure why she came back and did what she did, so Mason is going to have you dream walk Kayla to see what you can find out about her, Ian, and a very special ring."

"So, you are the one who stole Ian's ring? And you gave it to Mason? How do you expect us to believe you are on Ian's side, much less all of ours? You could be just using us like you have done this entire time with your lies," Brayden interrupts Maria's explanation of what is going to be expected of him and his powers.

"Yes, I took Ian's ring. Again, I have been doing everything that I can to gain Mason's trust. There is so much more that you do not understand about Mason. I would have never brought the ring here, if Kayla were not here. It is clear that she is destined to get the ring, somehow in the future, so bringing it here just increases her chances of getting it. Don't you agree?

Now, please listen to what I was trying to tell you, before you rightfully cut me off. When you dream walk Kayla, and you WILL have to do it, there is no getting around this part, there are several areas you will be able to be truthful. These will be the perfect places for you to build your base line for truths. This means you will have to use the same heart rate and breathing rhythm when you are asked a question you have to lie about, so it matches your baseline for the truth. Do you understand what I am talking about?"

"I understand you, but I have a question. Will I be telling more truths, or more lies?"

"Well, lies obviously. Why do you ask?"

"Because if I am going to have to tell more lies, than truths wouldn't it make better sense, if I set my baseline for the truth as the baseline for a lie? Like, if he asks me a truth first, but I tell my mind it's a lie, then my baseline is set to a lie, so when I have to lie, I don't have to try so hard. I will only have to focus on making the truths seems like a lie to me," Brayden explains to Maria.

"Do you think you will be able to do that consistently?"

"Why not? If you are expecting me to do it for just the opposite way, then this would be the most logical plan of action for his questions. Don't you agree?" Brayden questions Maria.

"His way does sound like it would give him less opportunities to slip up with Mason," Maclaine gives his opinion on Brayden's suggestion.

"If you believe in yourself, then I believe in you as well. Now let's get into the areas you can tell the truth and the areas where you will have to lie. Are you ready?" Maria needs to make sure Brayden is one hundred percent ready and sure he can pull this off before they begin. "Once we start, we won't have time for many questions, because I don't know exactly how much time I have down here alone with you. If I don't go back up to Mason soon, I may not be able to stop him from coming down here himself for his interrogation of the two of you. Understood?"

"Yes! I'm ready! Let's get this going."

***

"Garrett? The Garrett that has taken over my body and made me break into Mason's office, then open his locked safe to steal a ring? Then the same person that made me hide under Mason's desk, because he came back and almost caught us? The same Garrett that then left me with him and the stolen ring from the safe?" Kayla questions with a hint of shock.

"Yes, I am that same person. I told you that we have met before, but not in a traditional way," Garrett tells Kayla as he begins to stand her up on her own two feet.

As Kayla stands on her own now, she remembers more about Garrett. "You are also the one that took over that guard's body, the one while I was in the restroom, to tell me about Sebastian's half-sister. What even happened to that guard? Please, don't tell me that something bad happened to him because of what you did," Kayla demands of Garrett.

"Nothing bad happened to the guard. Actually, I was able to get him to knockout the other two guards that were escorting him down to the cells in the basement, once we got on the elevator. Once they were no longer a threat, I was able to lead the guard out of the compound undetected. We went several miles away from here, to a gas station. After we arrived at the gas station, we went into the bathroom there, and I had a conversation with him. I addressed him while looking into the bathroom mirror, so he could see himself speaking to himself, in a manner of speaking. I explained to the guard that he could never go back to the compound again, or try and reach out to anyone here, because no one would believe his story. I also suggested for him to make a clean slate of his life from that moment on. I also told him that if everything goes as it is supposed to, he would be a part of Mason's group again, if that is what he really wants. After that, I left his body, there alone in the gas station bathroom."

"Then how do you know that he is okay?"

"Because if Mason had already found the guard by now, he would not have us searching the entire compound, over and over again for him. So, I can safely assume that the guard took my advice and made a new start in life, one without Mason in it."

"Well, that is at least someone that was able to leave here and have a fresh start. I have no clue how long I planned on keeping myself with Mason. I left myself no clue, or memory of when, or how I am supposed to finally leave here."

"What do you mean, you left yourself no clues, or memories?"

"Oh, my future-self gave me memories before leaving me with Mason. She said some of the memories would be real, while others would be false, that were planted in my mind for my protection. So far, they have worked each time I have been in a position to answer a question that could be dangerous for me to answer truthfully. So, I kept thinking that there must be a memory implanted in my mind by Alexis, or myself from the future to help me. I have not been able to find anything about leaving here though. These memories just come to me when they are actually meant to be used."

"So, you, Alexis, left yourself, Kayla, here with Mason and he knows that Alexis is you from the future? What does he think about all of this?"

"That's just it. Mason doesn't think. He believes that Alexis is someone who has lied about everything, so he has betrayed her. He said he does not believe she is from the future at all. He believes that she is not me and nothing that she has told him will come true. And please don't ask me what she told him, because she didn't tell me."

"You mean to tell me that Mason, the person that is dead set on finding a watch that can go back in time, can't believe that Alexis is actually from the future? How is that even possible? He has dedicated his entire life to the fact that he thinks he can go back in time, making him from the future. But for him not to believe YOU can come back from the future as Alexis is ridiculous."

"Why don't you go and tell him that, since you are the one here with a choice. You should know why he can believe in going back to the past, but others can't from the future, even though if he were to go back in time, he would be the one from the future."

"Remember, I am not here by choice either. This is just the time in history I was assigned to observe and report about. But after reading about this period in history, I knew it had been changed and it is wrong. That is the only reason I had to step in and break the rules. If anyone from my time finds out that I did this, they would not only suspend me, but also fail me. But there is no way I can do an honest report on this time in history, if it's been altered. I have a suspicion this is happening because of someone from my time. The only thing is, I can't go back to my time to find out, because like you, I am stuck here until I finish my History Assignment."

"I'm sorry. I didn't know you were stuck here too. I thought you could go home whenever you wanted. If you can't go back until this is done, how will you find out if it is someone from you time?"

"Glad you asked. Do you remember when we were stuck under Mason's desk in his office, just after we stole the ring from his safe? You heard him speaking to himself, just as I did. I am beginning to think he was not speaking to himself, but more to someone who was in his body, as I was in yours. It really is the only way that Mason would have been having so much luck with everything he has accomplished. Now the question remains, if it is someone from my time, are they here because of me or because of Mason?"

"What do you mean by that? Why would someone from your world and time care about this place and time? The only logical assumption is that they are here because of you."

"That is the best conclusion for what we have been able to gather, but I can't afford to leave anything to chance. I will assume everything until I find out more."

"Agreed. So now that we have actually met, what do we do now? Will we see each other again, once we part ways today? And if we do see each other, will we pretend not to know each other, in other words, the same as always?"

"For now, I think it is best if we keep this meeting between just the two of us. I think the fewer people with information about us knowing each other in any way, will be the safest thing for us. We need to figure out how many pieces of this puzzle are actually out there, figuratively speaking that is. We need to find out who is working with us, and who is against us."

"That is true. With the way you have been going around and taking over bodies, it's hard to tell who themselves is really, or if they could be you," Kayla giggles at her last comment.

"Very cute, Kayla. I have only intervened, by using other peoples' bodies, when it has been absolutely necessary," Garrett replies. "I never did it for the fun of it, or for a good laugh. It has always been for the greater good."

"I am just joking with you, Garrett. Why are you so serious?"

"Sorry. I came here to observe this time period and give a report on what I learn for a grade in my History class in school, but it has turned into so much more than that now. I am having to help history correct itself, while also having to interact with others in this time period, or what we consider history, even though I was never meant to. Now, there is more riding on my mission than just a report. I have doubts within myself that I can't do what is needed to be done to make everything right again and that scares me more than any grade I can get."

"Why does that scare you so much? To you it would be just a grade, either pass or fail. It's not like you would actually have to remain here for the rest of your life and live this new life which you say we are living."

"Because the people that I meet here and become friends with changes things completely. I will have to live the rest of my life, knowing that the historic period was changed, and I was unable to correct it. My name could even be mentioned in this history timeline, now that it will be changed if I do too much intervening. This is why I am so scared, or at least one of the reasons I am scared."

"Oh, I see. That could cause a problem if you end up writing a report on this time period of history and you just happen to be in it. That would be very hard to explain to your teacher, or anyone really. You said one reason, so what would be another reason for you to be so scared?"

"That is something we will have to talk about at another time. Right now, I have to go back down to the basement cells, the ones where Brayden and Connor are being held. I was not supposed to be gone this long. I slipped out of the basement just as someone else was exiting the elevator. They got off and I slid in the elevator to come up to my room to grab something I may need later. If it was Mason that was in that elevator, he is going to ask Maclaine where I am, and I don't want to put Maclaine in harm's way with Mason."

"Then you better go. The only reason I have my own free time is because Maria showed up and needed to speak to Mason, alone as always. There is no telling what they are talking about, or scheming up now."

"I hate to leave you now, after finally getting to meet you, in my own body this time."

"Same here, but you cannot compromise the future, for your sake. I, on the other hand, once was in this present timeline, but now I am gone. The only thing I can do is put myself back in it. No harm, no foul, right? Now you, you are not even supposed to be here at all, so you are showing up in either of our histories would be a very bad thing."

"You are always right. Then I will have to say goodbye for now. But I hope to meet you again, in your proper timeline," is the last thing Garrett says to Kayla as he turns and walks down the long, bare, grey hallway, leaving Kayla standing alone at his barracks door.

Kayla stands at Garrett's door, lingering behind as Garrett makes his way down and out of the hallway. Once he is out of her sight, she slowly begins her own walk back out of the, now not so mysterious, hallway. While walking and thinking of everything Garrett and she talked about, she places her hands into her pants pockets. This is when she feels the small package she had placed in her right pocket, the small box she found in the entrance sitting room of this compound of Mason's. The small box that was next to the chair Maria was occupying, after she arrived with Connor and Brayden.

Kayla decides that now is as good of a time as any to remove the small box she found and open it, to see what is hiding inside of it. Kayla removes the small red box from her right pants pocket. The box has no wrapping on it or writing of any kind, just a lid that could slide right off. Kayla hesitates for a moment, because the more she learns about Maria, the less she trusts anything that may have been left for her, or by HER for someone else. But then she thinks, *What if this was left for Maria, but she never found it? This could be just what we need to find a way out of here and a way to stop Mason's plans.* With Kayla's sound logic, she quickly removes the lid from the top of the small red box.

Now that the lid is removed from the box, Kayla is surprised as to what she is seeing inside of it. *Why would anyone leave this for anyone?* Kayla wonders to herself. Then something clicks inside her mind about something that Garrett had just told her at his barracks door. His words to her were, "We need to figure out how many pieces of this puzzle are actually out there, figuratively speaking that is."

Could his comment and what is in the box just be a coincidence?" Kayla wonders out loud, as she is staring down into the opened red box, which contains only one single puzzle piece in it. Then she replaces the lid back on the small red box and places it back into her pants pocket. "Now I really don't know what, or who, to trust," she says in a soft sad whisper to herself, as she begins to go back to her room.

To Kayla, her free day is officially over.

Chapter 11

Time Ripples?

Still at the Believer's mansion, Jax knows that he does not have much time to find a place to use as a portal, but he has to find some place that will be large enough for him to walk through at least. As Jax is walking around, he spots a large pond in the back of the mansion. He makes the decision that this will be the perfect place for the portal.

Now that his location for a portal has been determined, Jax begins to memorize the entire area around him. He knows he is going to have to describe to Kenzie in great detail, for her to relay the same information to Ian, so he can focus on creating the portal in the pond. Jax is standing at the pond, looking in all directions, taking in as much of his surroundings as he possibly can. He knows he is only going to get one shot at creating this portal with Kenzie and Ian.

***

Ian and Kenzie run out of the front doors of the school just in time to stop their ride from leaving without them. Ian grabs the back-door handle of the

2017 Altima, which is what the app said would be arriving for them. Once they are both settled in the backseat, Kenzie closes the car door.

"It says here that you are going to 2800 Post Oak Boulevard. Is this correct?" the driver asks.

"Yes, we want to go to Gerald D. Hines Waterwall Park for an evening stroll. How long will it take you to get us there? We are in a bit of a hurry," Ian replies.

"As long as there are no accidents, we should be there in about sixteen minutes, give or take a few minutes."

"Great, thanks. Then let's get a move on."

Ian whispers to Kenzie, so the driver can't hear, "Okay, Kenzie, can you reach out to Jax and give him an update on our time to arrive? He needs to know just how much time he has left to find a place for me to make a portal."

"Give me a minute to reach out and make a connection with Jax," Kenzie whispers back to Ian.

Jax? Can you hear me? It's me, Kenzie. Kenzie waits for a moment for a reply. *Jax?*

Yes, Kenzie, I can hear you loud and clear. Why are you yelling anyway? Is something wrong? Jax answers her back.

I'm not yelling. And no, nothing has happened except we are about sixteen minutes from making it to the Waterwall. That's all the time you have left to find a suitable place to portal.

Then you are in luck, because I have already found the perfect place, Jax returns.

Great, then sit tight. I'll be contacting you again as soon as we are in a position to do what needs to be done without being seen.

"Okay, Jax says that he has already found the perfect place on his end, so when we get to the

Waterwall, it will then be left up to me. It will all depend on if I am going to be good enough to describe where he is, in such detail that you will be able to create a portal where he is and not in some public swimming pool full of kids," Kenzie quietly fills Ian in as they make their way to the Waterwall Park in their ride-share transportation.

"You will do just fine, Kenzie. As much as you like to talk, I'm sure you will be able to listen and relay in complete detail exactly where Jax is," Ian says with a quiet voice and a small giggle.

"Very funny, Ian. I don't talk that much, do I? Don't answer that!"

"You win. I won't answer your question, since we both already know the answer," Ian jokes with Kenzie as they continue on to Waterwall Park.

***

After informing Maria that he was not going to be able to join her, right now anyway, Mason waits for her elevator doors to close before walking away. He begins his way to his office, which is only a few doors down from the elevator. As he arrives at his destination, he reaches his hand out to grab the knob to his office door, then all of a sudden, his reach stops short of the knob.

What are you doing? Why are you keeping me from entering my office? Mason thinks to his body guest.

I think you should go down with Maria right now, his visitor thinks back to Mason.

Has something changed in the future that I need to know about, by not going down to the cells with Maria right now?

No. Not that I can see. I just don't understand your need to be alone at this moment, while Maria is down there in the cells questioning those prisoners. That's all.

Then if that is the only reason you have for me not going is because you don't understand, then release my arm and don't come back until you have some useful information for me.

With that statement from Mason, his body guest is gone, and Mason has control back over his own body again. Mason is now able to continue his reach for the knob for his office door, taking hold of it and gives it a quick twist and slight push to make his way into his office.

Mason quickly enters his office and closes the door behind him. Now that he has made it into his office, he begins to relax. Mason knows that no one will dare enter his office without knocking and announcing themselves first.

Now that Mason has shaken the edge off, he begins to move over to his safe. There are a few items that Mason stores in it for safekeeping, of course. Being that today is a special day for Mason, he opens the safe, once the safe door light turns green. With an open safe, Mason reaches in and retrieves the old journal he has been keeping stored inside the safe for many years now.

Mason turns and leaves the safe door open, and walks over to his desk, pulls back his chair, takes a seat and places the old journal on the top of his desk. He looks at the journal without opening it, just as he has done for twenty years. He already knows what's inside of it. He knows the outcome will be the same as it is every year when he does open it to read. The outcome never changes, just like it doesn't when he takes out the old coins, lock of hair, or even a photo of the family, which he has left all in the safe today.

Each of the other objects in his safe have a separate special day of their own, just like today is his mother's journal. Today, Mason remembers the day his mother left his life. He knows now she did not leave, or die during birth, but was taken from him. His time of living with the Believers was when he learned of Sebastian and Grayson's fights and the number of times Sebastian went back in those memories he stored in the Time Keeper to change the outcome of their fights. This is when he also learned of what a time ripple is. He figured out that every time Sebastian went back and saved his and Grayson's friendship, he caused time ripples.

Mason thinks back to when he first learned about time ripples from the Believers. Once he left the Believers, he went back to his old home one last time. The home he ran away from, this time came back to, to try to satisfy a strange feeling he has been struggling with his entire life. Mason broke into his father's apartment late that evening when he left the Believers. Mason knew it would be simple, because his father was either at his favorite watering hole, or passed out on the couch. Either way he knew he could get in and out without incident.

Mason was in luck. His father wasn't home, so he must be at the bar he loved so much. Mason began searching in his father's bedroom first. Even though he did not know what he was looking for, he figured he would know it once he found it. Mason went through his father's entire closet, dresser drawers, and even under his bed and still came up empty handed. Nothing he found, or touched soothed that aching feeling he had deep within himself. Starting to get upset, Mason began to wonder if there could be anything hidden under the floorboards, not only in his father's bedroom, but in the entire apartment. With that thought in his mind, he began to slowly walk around his father's bedroom, listening to any small sound or crackle the floor may cause if it may have had a hiding place under it. After pacing around his father's room for thirty minutes, which seemed like an hour or more to Mason, he decided to search in another room.

Mason made sure everything in his father's room was left in the same place it was in before he began his search, for whatever it is he was searching for. Not that he was afraid that his father would even notice if anything were moved, but mainly for his own self-preservation. As Mason searched for that 'something' that could relieve the pressure he felt inside, he was not going to feel the guilt of leaving a mess when it wasn't necessary. Now that the bedroom is back to its original mess, he heads to the living room, which is the next logical place for Mason to look.

Mason begins with the most obvious places, like the coffee table, the couch, under the couch, and still nothing. He checks the bookcase which runs along under the living room window. This is the same bookcase that is filled with all of Mason's childhood books. He can't believe that his father would keep all of the books he read as a child. Mason starts pulling out each book, so he can check the back of the bookcase for a false back, or a trap door, when all of a sudden, his favorite childhood book catches his attention. The book had landed on its spine, on the floor when he tossed it out of the bookcase, which caused it to open when it landed on the floor. What really catches Mason's eye is that fact that the inside of the book is hollow, and it wasn't hollow when he was a small boy reading it.

"Why would my father hollow out a book?" Mason thinks to himself out loud.

Mason reaches over and picks up the hollowed-out book. With a closer look, he can see there are some things inside of it. The contents of the book are a lock of hair, a small old journal, some old coins, and a photo of a family. Holding that photo in his hand, sends confusion through Mason's body. "This can't be real," Mason says out loud in disbelief.

Mason can't help but stare at the people in the picture that he just found in the hollowed-out book. The photo is of a family. The family consists of a mother, father, two small boys, and a small girl. The mother in the photo is holding a small journal, the same small journal that is now part of the contents of this book. He then notices that one of the small boys is holding the old coins. That left only three of the others with nothing in the book with the photo.

Mason did not have to look at the photo too long to realize that one of the small boys is him, and the man in the photo is his father. This leaves him to conclude that the lock of hair in the book belongs to the little girl in the photo. The photo is black and white, but Mason has a feeling he is correct. The only problem for Mason now is, "Who are these other people?"

Now that Mason has found what he thinks has caused this unsettling feeling inside of himself for so long, he quickly gathers the items that were hidden inside the hollowed-out book, places them back inside of it and closes it. After he sets the book aside, he places all the other books back on the bookcase. Mason is unsure when his father will return, so he wants to make sure he is gone before his father does come home. He places all the books back except his favorite one, which has been hollowed-out and filled with four separate types of objects. Mason then sneaks out as if he were never there.

Mason's trip down memory lane has given him perspective over the years, where he has figured out who the other people in the photo are. He believes he has also figured out when they were taken away from him, due to time ripples. There are dates on the back of the photo. Directly behind each of the three missing people in the photo is a corresponding date. Mason believes that the date on the back of the photo is the date each one disappeared due to a time ripple. Today is special because it is the date his mother was taken away by a time ripple, and this journal and the photo are all that are left of her.

When the date comes for the old coins, he will pull them out and remember his brother. And then the date of the lock of hair, which he now believes is that of his baby sister. As she was so small in the photo, this lock of hair must have been from her first haircut. He will pull them out on their dates in remembrance of each of them for their day. But today it is his mother's day.

Mason has decided that today he will open his mother's old journal, slowly and very gently. He is not sure how old the journal is, or how his mother not being here may affect the journal. He is not sure what he is expecting to find this year, but deep down, he really hopes to find more journal entries after today or the words changed. So far, each year his mother's last journal entry is the same.

I am not sure what tomorrow holds for me, but I can say that I have a perfect life. As a woman, I have the perfect husband and father to our three beautiful children. If there has been one thing I have learned from being married to Robert, it is that time can be taken from you at any time, so we live our lives to the fullest as we can. We have never put off until tomorrow what we can do today, because tomorrow is not a guarantee, but we only have right here and now.

If anything happens to me tomorrow, the one thing I would want you all to remember is that you can't let the past consume you. You will have to move forward with your lives, just as if the next day is not guaranteed, like your father and I did. This will be the only way you will have no regrets in life. You will have a life full of love, laughter, tears, smiles, friends, and even some failures. There is nothing wrong with failing, because you tried. Not trying will guarantee a failure, while trying will give you the opportunity to succeed. If you fail, learn from your mistakes, and try again, but keep trying and moving on.

I love you all and while this is just a precaution, I would regret not writing this, and you now know how I feel about regret.

See you all in the morning,
Love

Mom
(Tracy)'

No matter how many times Mason reads his mother's final journal entry, he has never taken her advice. He has no want to move forward with his life, he wants to go back and try to change it to get what was taken from him. He wants the life he was given, but taken away from him. He does not want to go back for wealth, fame, or notoriety, he wants to get his family back, even though he does not remember them. He wants it to replace the horrible memories of the way his father raised him alone.

Chapter 12

Truth/Lie?

Garrett continues through the lobby, as he exits the hallway from his barracks, on down to the hallway that will take him to the elevators, which will take him back down to the basement cells. Now that he has stopped thinking about Kayla, he's reminded that someone is already down in the basement with Maclaine, Brayden, and Connor. For all he knows, Mason could have already made his way down there as well.

With all of the possible scenarios running through his mind, Garrett almost walked past the elevators completely. After realizing where he was, he turns and without another thought, presses the call button. He knows he is going to have to go down there, one way or another, so he decides to waste no more time. He has to find out who all is down in the cells, and figure out a way to explain his absence.

The elevator arrives, and as its doors begin to open, Garrett hears Maria's voice inside of the elevator. She must be on the phone, or coming up with someone, either way, Garrett sees an opportunity. Quickly, he jumps to the side of the elevators, without being seen. Garrett hides in wait, then he sees Maria getting off the elevator alone. She is talking on her phone, which does not surprise him. Once Maria turns to walk in the opposite direction from where Garrett is hiding, he takes the opportunity to run and slip into the elevator before the doors close. *This could not have worked out more perfect, even if I had planned it myself,* Garrett thinks to himself with a big smile on his face.

Garrett presses the basement button and stands back against the elevator wall. Pleased with himself, he has forgotten that Mason still may be down in the basement. Just because Maria came up alone, doesn't mean that Mason never went down. "Oh, my, gosh! What am I supposed to do now?" Garrett says to himself out loud. With that thought, he moves from the back wall of the elevator to the side with the doors.

As the elevator stops on the basement level, Garrett is so snug up against the walls with the doors waiting for them to open, he doesn't realize they begin to slide open. Startled, he listens to see if he can hear Mason's voice, or anyone else's down in the basement. To his surprise, the only voices he hears are Maclaine's, Brayden's, and Connor's. They are all alone.

Breathing a relaxing breath, Garrett walks off the elevator and places on his night vision goggles and walks over to the other three. "Hey, so what did I miss while I was gone? Anything important?" Garrett jokes with the group.

"Let's see, did you know that Maclaine and Maria are working together?" Brayden answers back.

"I'm sorry, but what did you just say?"

"You heard me correctly. Maria and Maclaine are working together and have been this entire time. You mean to tell me that you didn't know?"

"Maclaine? Is this true? Are you and Maria working together, and if you are, to what end?" Garrett questions Maclaine.

"Well, if you would have stayed around a little bit longer, you would already know all the details. Speaking of sticking around, what was so important that you had to leave in the first place? Did anything happen to you while you were gone that we need to be aware of?" Maclaine fires back at Garrett.

"That is beside the point at the moment. Did you come up with a way to convince Mason that Brayden will be telling the truth?"

"As a matter of fact, Brayden came up with something that we believe will work. So, now it's your turn."

"Yes, I was able to make it to my room with no incidents to grab what I needed. Now, leaving my room to come back was a bit more complicated."

"What happened when you left your room, or while you were headed back that could make things complicated?" Maclaine asks.

"Well, when I was exiting my room, I didn't know it, but someone else was on the other side of my door. They had their hand on the door knob at the same time that I did, so when I pulled my door open, someone fell into my arms," Garrett replies to Maclaine.

"Who fell into your arms, Garrett?" Now Connor is joining the conversation.

"Yes, please do tell. Did Mason fall into your arms, or was it another guard?" Brayden interjects.

"Very funny, Brayden. No, Mason did not fall into my arms, but Kayla did. For some reason she was down at the end of the hallway to the barracks, and was about to go into my room. She was holding the knob at the same time I was, so when I pulled it open, she fell forward. I caught her before she could fall on the ground right in front of me."

"Did you tell her anything about how we are working with Maria? Or anything of our plans thus far?" Maclaine is desperately asking Garrett.

"No, I didn't reveal anything about our activities, or connection we have with Maria. I figured it would be best if she didn't know until the very last moment, when we need her. She will do no one any good if she starts acting different to Mason and Maria, or even towards you or me," Garrett clears up his reasons for keeping Kayla out of the loop.

"Perfect. Then you and I are on the same page. Now that we have that all cleared up, how about we fill you in on what we have come up with so far, while you were off flirting with Kayla," Maclaine tells Garrett.

"I was not flirting, first of all, but yes, why don't you fill me in on the plan. Anything will be better than this conversation," Garrett finishes.

With that, Maclaine begins to explain the plan they came up with, or more like the one Brayden came up with. They all start talking, while Garrett listens.

***

"Hello? Chancellor? So far, everything is going as planned. I just left Brayden and Connor, and they are now updated on what Maclaine and I have been planning," Maria tells the Chancellor on her cell phone as she is riding up the elevator from the basement.

Maria listens to what the Chancellor has to tell her, until the elevator reaches the main floor. As Maria exits, she begins to speak again.

"Brayden actually was able to come up with an even better plan than the one I had come up with in the beginning. I believe his way is going to be much more believable with Mason," Maria replies as she has made her exit off the elevator and is making her way to Mason's office. "Yes, I am headed there now. I hope he will take my word for it, so we can just skip to Kayla. I have to let you go. I am about to be at Mason's office door. I'll call you again the next chance I get. Good luck," Maria tells Chancellor Billie June as she hangs up her phone.

Maria slides her phone into her purse before knocking on Mason's office door. She gives his door three hard knocks and announces herself. "Mason, it's me, Maria. May I come in?" She knows to wait for an answer before entering Mason's office.

"Give me just a minute please," Mason replies to Maria. Now he knows that his time with his mother's journal has come to an end. He stands up from his desk, pushing his chair back. Once Mason is standing, he gently closes the journal and picks it up. Mason begins his walk over to his open safe, then places the journal inside with the other three objects and closes the door. Now that the safe door is closed, he turns the handle until the light turns from green to red, letting him know the safe is locked.

With the journal secure along with the other items, Mason turns and walks over to the door of his office, where Maria is waiting outside. Mason stands at the door for a moment to make sure he has his composure, then grabs the handle and gives it a turn, while pulling it open. In front of him, there stands Maria.

"Hello, Mason. Is this a bad time?" Maria questions.

"No, your timing couldn't have been more perfect. Come in and take a seat. I would like to hear how your meeting went with those two in the basement cells," Mason ushers Maria into his office.

"Thank you, Mason," Maria replies as she walks through his open door and makes her way to the nearest chair. She is in luck that the chair is right in front of Mason's desk, beside another chair.

Mason closes his office door behind Maria after she enters. Once his door is closed, he turns and walks over to the empty chair that is beside Maria, as opposed to his empty chair at his desk. As he sits, he asks Maria, "So, how are Garrett and Maclaine doing convincing Brayden and Connor into helping us?"

****

As Ian and Kenzie pull up to Gerald D. Hines Waterwall Park, Ian has Kenzie contact Jax to let him know that they will be in place very soon.

Jax, are you ready? Kenzie thinks to Jax.

Yes, I'm in place and ready. Do you want me to start describing my location to you now? Jax thinks back to Kenzie.

No, not yet. I am just giving you a heads up that we are pulling up to our destination now. We still need to make sure that it is clear of people. I'm sure you will agree that we don't want a lot of people watching Ian create a portal and you coming through it.

I didn't think of that. Okay, you two do whatever you need to do, and let me know when the coast is clear, Jax finishes as his connection with Kenzie is released.

"Jax is ready when we are. Now all we have to do is get across this park to the Waterwall and make sure there are no people around. By the way, what is your backup plan, in case there are tourists at the Waterwall?" Kenzie asks Ian.

"What do you mean, 'backup plan?' We are going to use the Waterwall regardless of if there are people there or not," Ian replies to Kenzie.

"Have you lost your mind? You are not going to be able to create a portal in the water that is rushing down the Waterwall in front of people. That will surely be noticed and possibly reported to the police, which would get back to the school."

"Relax, Kenzie. Who said I was going to use the water side of the Waterwall to create the portal? I am going to try something a little different this time. Right now, we need to get across this park and behind the Waterwall," Ian surprises Kenzie as they exit the back of the ride-share they have taken to Waterwall Park.

"Whatever you say, Ian."

"Trust me. When have I ever let you down?"

Kenzie gives Ian a quick look, but does not answer that last question. Instead, she takes Ian's lead, and they begin to jog across the park towards the actual Waterwall on the South end of the park.

The park is not as busy as either of them had expected it to be, which could be part of it being a week day and before five o'clock. The closer they make it to the Waterwall, the more people they notice inside the structure. They both walk through the middle opening to go inside the Waterwall, and can already see at least twenty people inside the semicircle, massive wall that stands sixty-four feet tall. Ian knows he is going to have to have to try his alternative way to make a portal for Jax to come through.

"Follow me," Ian tells Kenzie as he turns to the right and begins to walk along the wall on the front side of the structure. As they are walking towards the end of the interior of the Waterwall, Kenzie secretly contacts Jax.

Jax, I'm not sure how this is going to work out. Ian is not going to use water, or any reflective surface to create the portal this time. He is taking us to the backside of the Waterwall. There is no water back here, or mirrors, so I don't know how he is going to be able to create a portal back here! Kenzie thinks to Jax.

Am I hearing you correctly? Did you just say that Ian is going to try to make a portal without using water or a reflective surface of any kind? Jax thinks back to Kenzie.

Yes, that is what I said. I will fill you in with more details when he tells me more, Kenzie tells Jax as she breaks off her connection with him and turns her focus back to Ian. "Where are we going?"

"I told you, I have something new I want to try, but we need to be behind the structure where the water is actually flowing down on the other side," Ian explains to Kenzie.

"You mean to tell me that you have not tried this new method before, and this is going to be the first time you do? How sure are you that this is even going to work?" Kenzie asks Ian in disbelief.

"I'm pretty sure it will work. Now that we are in position, go ahead and contact Jax and begin to repeat his description of his location to me, so we can try and get this started," Ian directs Kenzie, as they are standing on the backside of the Waterwall, at Waterwall Park at the Galleria in Houston.

Kenzie does as she is told. *Jax, we are now ready for you to begin describing your location to me, and then for me to repeat it to Ian. Are you ready?*

I'm as ready as I will ever be, Jax thinks back to Kenzie. *So, let's begin, shall we?*

Jax begins to describe the field he is standing in, which is behind the mansion of the Believers. He tells Kenzie, in great detail, about the tree lines that run along the North and West ends of the field. Now that he has painted a picture of the field itself to Kenzie, he turns his focus on the actual pond. He best describes the shape of it to look like the big island of Hawaii, Kona. The water is also oddly a clear bright blue, like you would see in Hawaii and not in a pond in the middle of a field.

Ian closes his eyes as Kenzie repeats, word for word, the description Jax has been thinking to her. As Kenzie keeps repeating Jax's words, Ian extends his hands out in front of him. He looks as if he is reaching for the wall of the back of the Waterwall. Kenzie keeps on repeating Jax's words to Ian.

"What is that?" Kenzie asks Ian, who does not open his eyes, nor answer her. "The back of the wall is starting to open up in a circular motion."

Jax, what is happening on your end? Anything?

Yes actually. There is a swirl forming in the pond. Is that the portal?

I'm not sure, but wait for me tell you when to jump if it is the portal.

"Ian? Jax has a portal opening in the pond where he is. When should he jump in?"

"NOW! But make sure he jumps in feet first!" Ian exclaims.

Jax, jump now, but make sure you go feet first. Do you hear me? Jump feet first right now! Kenzie expresses to Jax, but gets no response.

All of a sudden, Jax comes shooting out of the portal on the back of the Waterwall like he was just on a slide at a water park, but he is still dry.

"Jax!" Kenzie yells out loud. "You made it!"

"Yes, I did. Ian, you can close the portal now and open your eyes. You did an amazing job. Thank you both," Jax tells them.

"It's good to see you, Jax," Ian replies.

"Okay, now we need to get back to the school, so we can catch up and figure out what we are going to do next."

Chapter 13

A Day Off?

"I'm glad you asked, because that is the reason I have come here to see you," Maria informs Mason of her intentions.

"Really now? I hope you came here to tell me some good news," Mason replies back to Maria, as he leans back in his chair beside the one where Maria is sitting.

"Garrett and Maclaine have been using what they call, 'Need a Friend in Here,' method on Brayden and Connor, and it is working with very little resistance from either of them. Brayden and Connor both know they have no one here to trust, so if they have to trust someone, it may as well be two other young boys like them. They have now convinced the pair of them that cooperating with us is the only option they have. So, I would say, yes. It is good news that I bring to you."

"Well, now that does sound like great news, actually. After interrupting my free day with Kayla, you should be grateful that it is such good news. Now that we have them with us on our side, will Brayden be ready to complete his task?"

"It shouldn't be much longer. We haven't informed either of them about what we need them to do at this moment. Our main goal was to make sure they would turn to our side. Now that they have, we will now move on to phase two," Maria tells Mason, while holding back a small smile of relief, since Mason has not mentioned that he wants to question them and wants to just move forward instead.

"You have exactly four hours to prepare Brayden for his mission. I suggest you go back down to the basement and get to work. I am going to have one of the housekeepers go and freshen up the room that is next to Kayla's, for us to use with Brayden to try and dream walk Kayla tonight. Now, while you are down in the cells with them, I am going to go check on Kayla to see how her day went. Also, to make sure she is back in her room by now. Do you have any questions or concerns?"

"No, I believe you have made yourself perfectly clear. I will leave you now and head down with the others, while you do what you need to do. I will wait for you to either come get us, or summon for us to the room next to Kayla's," Maria replies to Mason with conviction in her tone.

"Let's hope you are able to do what you claim you can in the next four hours, or we will have to do things my way. And I can promise that no one will like my way. Now, am I still perfectly clear?" Mason reminds Maria of his power.

"Absolutely. We will be ready when you need us. I will make sure of that myself," Maria assures Mason as she is now standing in front of him. With a slight nod, Maria steps backward a couple of steps, then turns and walks the rest of the way to Mason's office door. Reaching for the door handle, she first has to unlock the door with her other hand, as Mason left the key in the door lock, after he closed it and locked it.

Now that Maria is out of Mason's office, she is very careful with her movements. She continues with her normal slow pace back to the elevators, so she can go back down and let the others know what's about to happen, and in only four hours. Also, as she slowly approaches the elevators she thinks, I need to speak to the Chancellor, but after that talk with Mason, I don't know of any safe places left to make a call.

Maria pushes back her thoughts and presses the call button for the elevator. She just needs to make sure Brayden will be ready for his mission, because if he isn't, they are all going to be sorry. That includes herself, from what she gathered from Mason's last comment. As Maria is thinking about the best way to approve them, the elevator arrives to her floor and the doors open. Of course, the elevator is empty upon arrival, so Maria makes her way inside.

Just as the doors are closing, Maria's phone starts to ring. As the ringing of her phone startles her, she reaches down and pulls out her phone from her purse. She can see by the caller ID that it's the Chancellor calling.

"Hello, ma'am. Forgive me, but I don't think now is the best time or place for us to communicate. I only have four hours to make sure Brayden is ready, plus I'm not sure where a safe place to talk freely is. I hope you understand?" Maria tells the Chancellor, on the other end of the phone.

Maria holds the phone to her ear for a few seconds, then lowers it down back into her purse. If words were exchanged, they were quick. Just as Maria drops the phone inside her purse, the elevator stops and its doors open, now on the dark basement floor. Maria takes a deep breath and exits the elevator into the darkness. When she released the phone in her purse, she had already grabbed her night vision goggles from there, and now is putting them on so she can see. Now she must give Maclaine, Garrett, Brayden, and Connor the news. They have to be ready in four hours, or less. They all know Mason is unpredictable.

***

"So? How was your visit with whoever you when to see? Were you able to get the answers to the questions that we can't?" Ian asks Jax as they are waiting for their ride-share to stop completely in front of the school.

"I will fill you in on where I have been going, and who I have been going to see and a lot more information once we are in the school. Is that fair?" Jax asks Ian and Kenzie.

"Can't I just sneak a little look inside your mind? Just for a second?" Kenzie asks Jax jokingly.

"Absolutely not, Kenzie. The things I have to tell you actually have more to do with Ian, so you could be confused and maybe disappointed at what you see," Jax snaps back to Kenzie. "Am I making myself clear?"

"Fine! You don't have to be so mean about it. I was only kidding," Kenzie expresses back to Jax.

After that, there was no more talking between the three of them, even after their ride stops at the school. Just as soon as their ride stops, Kenzie grabs the back door handle and opens it quickly, since she was on the sidewalk side. As the door flies open, Kenzie jumps out of the backseat of the car and begins to walk towards the school entrance. She is in no mood to listen to Jax right now.

After Kenzie is out of the car, Jax makes his way out, leaving only Ian to climb across the backseat and out of the back door. Once Ian is clear of the car door, Jax shuts it. Now Jax and Ian turn to start walking to catch up with Kenzie.

"Kenzie! Please stop for a moment. At least let us catch up with you," Ian shouts at Kenzie before she can make it into the school doors.

Kenzie does not look back, but she does stop to wait for Jax and Ian to catch up. She knows deep down that her only hope in finding her little brother, Connor, will be with their help. To her, he is the most important person, or plan, that she needs to worry about right now.

Jax and Ian reach Kenzie at the front doors of the school. She does not greet them, or show them any type of acknowledgement, she simply turns and opens the doors to the entrance. As Kenzie opens the doors and makes her way inside the school lobby, Jax and Ian follow suit. The three of them continue through the lobby, past the concierge desk, straight to the elevators. As they gather in the elevator foyer, Jax presses the call button.

"So, whose room are we going to this time?" Ian asks Jax.

"Whose room do you both prefer?" Jax replies, hoping to get a response from Kenzie.

"Kenzie, where would you rather go? You know, we don't have to go to a bedroom, but we could go to another room in the school. We can go anywhere you want to go. Anywhere that you will be comfortable to listen to what Jax has to tell us," Ian is asking Kenzie now.

"To be honest, I really don't care where we go. I am just ready to get my brother back. If Jax has something to tell us that will get us closer to getting Connor back, then we can talk in a bathroom for all I care. So, you pick a place and let's go, if you both don't mind," Kenzie replies.

"Then why don't we go to the Sky Lounge? It should be empty now, and even if anyone comes in, it's big enough for us to just move into another section of the room," Jax takes the lead.

Now that they all agree on a place, the elevator has arrived. Once the doors are open, the three of them step inside. First Kenzie enters, next is Ian, then pulling up the rear is Jax. As Jax enters, he turns to press the button to the top floor, but notices that Kenzie has already beat him to it. Jax knows why Kenzie is upset with him, and he knows that he will need to do something to help her get past this anger. Right now, they all need to be on the same page and working together, not holding grudges.

Kenzie? Are you out there, somewhere in this tiny elevator? Jax thinks to Kenzie. *I'm sorry that I snapped at you earlier. I am giving you permission to look into my mind now, if you want to, so you can get a head start on what we are about to talk about. I know how much of an eager student you are, so think of this as extra credit.*

Kenzie begins to laugh out loud in the elevator for Jax and Ian both to hear her. "Thank you, Jax, but I will wait. Besides, I have enough extra credit this year. But again, thank you," Kenzie tells Jax with her voice and not with her mind. Kenzie knows Jax is sorry, and she lets her anger go. To be honest with herself, being angry is harder than just being the nice person she always has been.

"You are welcome," Jax replies to Kenzie as he begins to laugh with her.

Ian is clueless as to what has just happened between the two of them, but he is happy to see they are friends again. Before Ian knows it, the elevator has already reached the twenty-fourth floor, which is where the Sky Lounge is located. The elevator stops, the door opens, and the three of them try to exit at the same time, unlike when they first entered the elevator in the lobby. *Things are back to normal, or as normal as they can be,* Ian thinks to himself with joy.

Now that Jax, Kenzie, and Ian are out of the elevator, they make a turn to the left in the foyer. With only a few feet to go, they turn left again to the door of the Sky Lounge. Jax takes a look through the window in the door, and to his expectations, the lounge is empty. Jax takes ahold of the door and pulls it open for Kenzie and Ian to go on in, and then he follows behind them after they pass through the door.

"Why don't we sit over on the far end of the lounge? The section that is farthest away from this kitchen and pool table area. This way if anyone does come in, these will most likely be the areas they will want to use," Kenzie suggests.

"Good thinking, Kenzie! It's good to have this Kenzie back!" Jax compliments her choice.

"I couldn't agree more. Now she and I can go back to thinking things about you, without you knowing about them," Ian laughs while nudging Kenzie.

"What was that you just said?" Jax asks Ian.

"Nothing. Shouldn't we get started?" Ian replies while winking at Kenzie.

"Yes, you are correct. I have a lot to tell you, and we have very little time. So, take your seats and I will get started," Jax tells Kenzie and Ian, as he hurries over to the area they have decided on using.

Now that they have all found a place to be comfortable for an hour or so, Jax begins.

✳✳✳

Once the door closes behind Maria, Mason knows he needs to go and check on Kayla. He has not seen her since Maria showed up and interrupted their free day on the shooting range. He actually feels bad that their day had been ruined. Mostly he felt bad for Kayla, since she really has no one here that she can consider a friend, which is why he gave her permission to roam freely around the grounds instead of making her stay in her room. Mason wants to go see how the rest of her day went and also to see if she will tell him anything useful.

Mason stands up from the chair he had been sitting in while talking to Maria. He knows he does not have to walk very far down the hall from his office to Kayla's room, as it is only a few doors down. Mason takes a stroll down the hallway, until he is standing in front of Kayla's bedroom door. He is not sure if she is even back from her free day, so he gives her door three soft knocks, then waits to see if she answers.

"Who is it?" comes Kayla's voice from inside her room.

"Hello, Kayla. It's me, Mason. Am I catching you at a bad time, or may I come in?"

With no response, Kayla walks over to her bedroom door and opens it up to find Mason standing outside, alone. "Yes, you may come in."

"Thank you. I wanted to come and see how your day went, since our free day was interrupted."

"It was fine, actually. I just walked around, went to the lobby and sat there for a bit, then got bored, so I came back to my room. I figured if I was going to be alone, I might as well be alone in here. At least I could take a nap if I wanted to."

"And did you?"

"And did I do what?"

"Take a nap? You said if you wanted to you could have taken one. I am merely wondering if you felt the need to want to take a nap today."

"Oh, no. I didn't. It really has been a very long day though. So, how was your day with Maria?"

"It was about the same as all of her meetings go. She seems to think what she has to say should override everything else anyone has planned, yet her information is nothing more than something that I could have waited another week to find out. So, let's say that my meeting with Maria was enough to want me to trade places with you for the day, because I would have taken a nap."

"That bad, huh? I sort of figured all your meetings with Maria were always of the utmost of importance. I cannot imagine you being bored with her around. She is for sure a character."

"You can say that again, but she can really wear you down to where you feel like you have nothing left at all. One of the best parts about having a meeting with Maria is when it is over, and she says 'Goodbye' and walks out the door."

"Now that's funny!"

"It's the truth. Well, I don't want to take up too much of your time, not this late in the evening. I really wanted to come and check on you to see how you were doing. I don't want you to think that I planned for Maria to show up and ruin our day together."

"I know you didn't plan that. From what I have learned, from the few times I've seen Maria, I know she never plans ahead but merely ruins other people's days. Why should today be any different? I'm sure she gets pleasure out of ruining other people's days."

"That sounds like a perfect description of Maria, if I do say so myself. Well, I don't want to keep you up too long. If you are fine with this evening, then I will still try to make it up to you."

"You don't have to do that. You had your boring day, and I had mine. Let's say we are even with the way our free day ended," Kayla tells Mason as they are still standing awkwardly across from each other at her bedroom door.

"Okay, agreed. Well, I will go ahead and leave you now. Like I said, I don't want to keep you up any longer than you want to be. I think it's time I went to my office and called tonight a night," Mason says to Kayla.

"Yes, maybe that will be best. Since I didn't take a nap, I am a bit tired. I may go to bed early tonight. Thank you for coming to check on me," Kayla agrees with Mason.

"If you need anything to eat before you go to bed, just press the intercom and the chef will prepare something for you. It will be no bother for him, and he will have it prepared in no time."

"That's sweet of you, but I think I will go take a hot bath, then get ready for bed. Never know what tomorrow holds for us."

"As you wish. Enjoy your bath. I'm going to my office to do a little work, before I call it a night for myself. Good night, Kayla."

"Good night, Mason."

With Kayla's 'Good night,' Mason removes himself from her room and then heads down the hallway to his office. From his office, he will be able to tell when Kayla goes to take her hot bath and when she finishes and heads back to her room to get ready for bed. That will be when Mason is ready to summon Maria and her team in the basement, to the room next to Kayla's. So, for now, he waits.

Chapter 14

Ring Origin?

Maria makes her way over to where Garrett and Maclaine are standing. "I need to talk to you two for just a minute," Maria tells the two of them as she reaches their location.

"Sure, what's going on?" Maclaine asks Maria.

"Come over here with me for a minute and find out," Maria snaps back.

The three of them walk over to the elevator foyer to be alone, so Maria can speak privately with them both.

"I just left Mason's office and told him what great progress you two have made with Brayden and Connor. I also told him that they trust you two, and we are now going to begin with Phase Two," Maria expresses to Maclaine and Garrett.

"And just what exactly is Phase Two?" Garrett asks either of the other two.

"I suppose this will be part of your plan, now that Brayden and Connor trust you, to make sure you can get them to do what we need them to do. In other words, we need to make sure that Brayden is ready to dream walk Kayla and also be able to lie to Mason with ease. Mason has given us four hours to get them ready. But if I know Mason, he will be calling for us before our time is up.”

“What do you mean, calling for us?” Maclaine asks Maria.

“Oh, yes, when Mason is ready for us, we will be going to the room next to Kayla’s. He believes that this will be the easiest way for Brayden to use his gift on Kayla. Also, this is going to be his way of having us all in the same place, if we fail,” Maria elaborates.

“That last part does not sound good to me. Is there something else you are leaving out?” Maclaine asks.

“Let’s not worry about any of that right now. Let’s focus on Brayden and if he is going to be able to pull this off. We might as well go and let Brayden and Connor in on the updated plan. I think we should leave out that last part. You know, the part I have not told you about if we fail. I don’t want to put too much pressure on Brayden,” Maria instructs Garrett and Maclaine.

With the end of Maria’s instructions, the three of them turn and make their way back around the corner, only to find that the cells are empty!

“Where are they? Did either of you let them out of their cells?” Maria is beginning to stress out.

“No, they have been in the cells the entire time we have been down here,” Maclaine answers.

“Obviously not, or they would be here now,” Maria states. “Find them. NOW!”

***

“The first thing you both need to understand about me is where I grew up. You see, Ian, you actually know a little bit about this. I was given up by my parents to become a Believer. I was taken to them at a very young age, to the home of the Believers. Once I was left there, I was raised in the house with other Believers and taught all the rules and laws of being a Believer. Kenzie, you may not know it, but I do have a code I have to follow, and I have rules I have to obey and even laws I cannot break. Well, the head Believer, that pretty much raised us all, is Chancellor Billie June.

Now, this is where things may get a little confusing. You see, before Chancellor Billie June was made Chancellor, she was once a young Believer, like I was when I was left at the house. Billie June was going to be assigned to be Sebastian Hele's watcher. But she made a choice that would end her chances of ever becoming Sebastian's watcher, or a watcher at all. Billie June broke not only a rule, but a law of our people. The only thing anyone ever knew about was the rule she broke, not the law," Jax takes a pause.

"What rule did Billie June break that would keep her from ever being a watcher?" Kenzie asks with a soft-spoken voice.

"She was unable to return the Time Keeper in time for Sebastian to be able to find it," Jax replies.

"What do you mean, return the Time Keeper? It was lost after that fight he and Grayson had, so we thought. But the vision I was shown had a little girl in it, who ran out from the shadows of the night, in that alley after the fight and picked up something. I knew it was the Time Keeper. So, you are telling me that the Chancellor Billie June, of the Believers, stole the Time Keeper that night?" Ian is asking the questions now.

"Yes, but before you get too upset Ian, she did have a reason for doing so. Which brings me to when she broke a law of our people. See, Billie June learned of Sebastian's half-sister, Camryn, so she took the Time Keeper to Camryn's family. This is when she took a small piece of the Time Keeper and dropped it into a pot of melted silver. Camryn's father, William, was a very well-known silversmith during that time and was making a silver ring to give to his wife, Jennifer on the day of Camryn's christening. William told Jennifer to make sure she gave that ring to Camryn, when she came of age. He also wanted to make sure the ring was passed down to only the females in their family bloodline," Jax stops for another quick break.

"Are you telling me that he knew Camryn wasn't his daughter and that she had connections to the Time Keeper, or the Helen bloodline?" Ian asks Jax.

"What is the law Billie June broke?" Kenzie asks while Jax is on story time break.

"First, to answer your question, Ian, no. William had no idea that Camryn was Jacob's child and not his own. She was his child in all aspects of life, as he raised her and never left her side, and knew no different. He knew the love he had for Camryn was real before she was even born, being of different bloodlines doesn't change that. William merely felt obligated to tell his wife Jennifer those things about the ring and passing it on. Which leads me to your question, Kenzie. The law Billie June broke was that she used her powers of suggestion on a mortal. Billie June gave the feelings William felt about the ring to him. We are never to use our gifts on mortals. Our gifts are only to be used to help someone of the Helen Family bloodline find the Time Keeper. This is why we now are the only ones who know what the ring is and how it came to be," Jax pauses.

"Is that it? Those are the only questions either of you have for me?" Jax asks surprised.

"Is that the end of what you have to tell us? Or is there more?" Ian replies to Jax.

"Well, this is the place that I have been going to and seeking information and advice from the Chancellor. There is more, but to be honest, I'm not even sure if I can explain some of the things she told me. Like the fact that your ancestor, Clint, stayed in the red room Junior showed you with the red wallpaper, large bed fit for a king, and the fireplace, before you were next shown the old classroom. The only thing is, your ancestor Clint never had the Time Keeper to store the memory in, but it still ended up in it somehow. Now, you see why I can't explain everything the Chancellor told me?" Jax explains.

"WOW! Are you serious? My ancestors stayed in a room at the house you grew up in, the house for Believers. Why would my ancestor be at the house of your people?" Ian asks Jax in disbelief.

"That in itself is an entirely different conversation, not meant for now. We need to stick to what I have already told you," Jax interjects.

"You mean back to the ring, don't you?" Kenzie asks.

"Yes, I do," Jax answers.

"Fine then. So, you said that William made a silver ring for his wife, Jennifer, to give to their daughter, Camryn, when she came of age. Now, that ring is also made from a small piece of the Time Keeper, which means..." Ian stops.

***

As Mason sits in his office waiting for any sign of Kayla going into the restroom, which is next to his office, to take her hot bath before bed, he can't help but stare at his safe. Thinking of the objects of a life he never had, but could have had. Then Mason is caught off guard by the slamming of the door next to his office. "Perfect timing," Mason says to himself out loud.

I wonder how long this is going to take. How long can a bath take in the first place? Mason thinks to himself.

That will be the last time Mason thinks that question to himself again, or out loud, after waiting for almost an hour to hear the bathroom door slam shut again. "Now, I just need to give Kayla enough time to fall asleep. Maybe I should go see if she would like some tea and put some sleeping powder in her drink. What am I talking about? I am not going to be that type of person. I will wait until she falls asleep on her own, before I have Brayden invade her mind," Mason says to himself in his office.

While Mason waits for Kayla to fall asleep, he summons one of his guards to his office. Mason thinks, *While Kayla falls asleep, now is the perfect time to bring Maria and the others from the basement and up to the room next to Kayla's.*

The guard arrives at Mason's office and receives his orders. Once he knows what he is expected to do, he turns and leaves Mason's office. The only thing the guard has to do is go down to the basement cells, and let Maria, Maclaine, and Garrett know Mason is ready for them to bring up Connor and Brayden to the room next to Kayla's. So, with his orders, the guard heads to the elevators.

***

"Relax, ma'am. We are right here," Brayden says with a laugh to Maria as he taps her on the shoulder. "Connor and I wanted to have a little fun while you three stressed out."

"How did you get out of the cells in the first place?" Maria asks.

"Well, Ms. Know-it-all, once Connor puts these night vision goggles on, he is able to see things in the dark, right? Well, that made it very easy for him to pick the locks on the doors to our cells, with his power, while y'all were standing over there talking. Now, what's the big deal? Mason is almost ready for us? That's a good thing, because I can assure you that Connor and I are tired of being down here in the dark. I will be able to do what needs to be done, and Mason will not even know," Brayden says with confidence.

"Well, why don't you both, get back into the cells, just in case Mason, or someone he sends to get us and sees you out of them right now," Maria suggests.

"Fine, if it will make you feel more comfortable. Connor let's get back in our cages. Also, thanks for picking the locks, we needed some fun," Brayden laughs with Connor as they step back into their cells.

"Now what? Are we just going to sit and wait?" Connor questions the group.

"Well, we could come up with a Plan B. Just in case things do not go as we anticipate. I would rather be over prepared than under," Garrett replies.

"Great, now what do you have in mind?" Maclaine asks.

The group begins to come up with a backup plan. The, now five of them, throw ideas back and forth for about an hour and a half. Then they hear the elevator stop on their floor, and they all get quiet.

Maria leaves Garrett and Maclaine to stand next to the cells, and walks over to the elevator. Maria is curious as to who is coming to get them. She knows Mason too well to know that it is time for them to head upstairs.

The elevator door opens, revealing one guard, no Mason, or a team of guards, just one, which lets Maria know that Mason believes what she told him earlier in his office. She told Mason that Brayden and Connor are going to be working on their side. That makes Maria relax, just a little.

"Can I help you?" Maria asks the guard.

"I have been sent down here by Mr. Mason. My orders are to retrieve all of you, and guide you to his location. So, grab the other four and bring them this way?"

"As you wish."

"Who is it?" Garrett asks Maria as she comes around the corner.

"Just as I figured. Mason is wanting us now, so he sent a guard to fetch us. I knew he could not wait for the four hours. But, his impatience is a weakness we can use later, if we must. Right now, open the cells and let them out, so we can head upstairs," Maria tells Garrett.

"No need to get us, we are right here and ready to go," Brayden says while popping up behind Garrett.

"Do you mind? Stop breaking out and sneaking up on people. It's creepy. It's not like we are keeping anything from either of you. We are depending on you…"

"That's enough, Garrett. Now, everyone calm down and follow me to the elevator where our guide waits for us," Maria's tone silences everyone. She has those leadership qualities that many seek but never find. What she has can't be taught, she was born with it. Maria was born to be a leader.

Maria, of course, takes the lead with Garrett, Brayden, Connor, and Maclaine in tow behind her. They head to the elevator.

"Is everyone here?" the guard asks Maria.

"Yes. Didn't Mason tell you how many people you were coming down here to fetch?"

"Mason told me five. Why do you ask?"

"Because you had to ask if we were all here. As you can see, there are five of us standing right in front of you. If you would bother looking at us."

"Sorry, ma'am. I have to ask because I am blind. Do you mind bringing each one of you in front of me, please? I want to make sure everyone is here."

"Please, forgive my rudeness. If I would have known…"

"You would have treated me differently? I prefer to see the real person I meet, not the one who has to act differently in front of me. But thank you for your honesty. Now, if you don't mind. Each person, one at a time, in front of me, please."

Without any other words from Maria, she first places Connor over in front of the guard, just as he asked. The guard reaches out his hands and begins to feel Connor's face, nose, mouth, dimples, and even his ears.

"What is your name?" the guard asks Connor.

"Connor. What is your name?"

Without answering Connor's question, he simply says, "Next please."

Next up is Brayden. The guard seems surprised by the age difference between Connor and the boy in front of him now. The guard continues the same process as he did with Connor. He asks his name as well.

"Brayden."

The guard continues with this process, until he is satisfied that there are five people now on the elevator with him. Once the guard is sure he has everyone he was sent to retrieve, he reaches his arm out to begin his search for the button to press, the elevator button for Mason's floor. "Once the elevator stops, I will need you all to follow me down the hall to the room Mason is waiting for you in, but I have to ask you to be extremely quiet. By the way, my hearing is impeccable, so one word or noise, and I will hear it. To prove my hearing abilities, it's not nice to sneak up on people Brayden," the guard means business.

When the elevator stops, the guard steps out first and does not wait to hear if the others are following him, because he can hear they are. They all walk down the hall, silently as possible, until they reach a door. The guard stops, turns, and opens the door without even knocking. As the door swings wide open, the group sees Mason.

"Come in, please. It's time we see what you can do, Brayden. The bed is for you, so the rest of you can get comfortable and get ready to watch the show," Mason commands.

Chapter 15

Dreams?

As Ian is sitting there in the Sky Lounge with his eyes and mouth wide open, Kenzie is just watching him.

"What is it, Ian? Why are you just sitting there? Did I miss something?" Kenzie is spitting out questions left and right. "Don't just sit there, say something, Ian!"

"Give him a minute or two to process what he just realized," Jax tells Kenzie, like it's no big deal that Ian is sitting like a statue.

"What are you talking about, Jax? Can you fill me in since I am unable to make any connections to whatever Ian has?" Kenzie asks.

"Just another minute, and Ian will tell you himself. Trust me, it's all catching up to him now."

"Why do you keep saying things like that? I'm so lost right now. I want to hear more about the ring," Kenzie asserts herself.

"The ring is part of the Time Keeper. That means that Sebastian's half-sister, Camryn, actually had access to the Time Keeper. That also means that every female on her side of the Hele bloodline, also had, and still do have, access to the Time Keeper as well," Ian begins to explain.

"Okay, so I get that, but what is up with the big statue moment?" Kenzie inquires.

"Because Kenzie. That also means that Kayla and I are related," Ian tells her in a soft tone.

With that information provided to her, Kenzie has no more questions. She is the one now sitting in the Sky Lounge of the school in statue mode.

Everyone just sits there, still in an empty room, processing everything they have either learned or have just been told.

"Okay, I have a question. How is any of this information supposed to help us find Kayla, Brayden, and Connor, right now?" Kenzie breaks the silence.

"I'm sorry?" Ian replies. "What exactly is that supposed to mean?"

"It's just a question. I want to know what we can do to get my brother, Connor, back. You remember him, don't you? Or have you forgotten about him and Brayden?" Kenzie lets out in a very loud and harsh tone.

"So, all of this with us being friends now is just so you can get your brother back? What about my family member who is missing from time? Is my family member not as important as yours? And by the way, remember she is also with Brayden and Connor, your brother," Ian spits out back to Kenzie.

Kenzie can't believe what she is hearing from Ian. Connor is the only thing she has left in her life, since everything else was ripped away from her. Her parents, home, school, and friends are all gone. She has nothing but her brother, Connor, and Ian wants to just dismiss her feelings. She wonders why he would do this to her. As Kenzie sits and just looks at Ian, with disbelief, her eyes begin to water up.

"Kenzie? I'm sure Ian did not mean any harm by his words to you. We both know getting Connor and Brayden back are our first steps in getting Kayla back. But please give him just a little slack. He just found out that his best friend is also his relative and is still missing. He is also just finding out that the connection they share with each other is so strong because of their bloodline. You both are going through a rough time right now, so please keep an open mind about his feelings too," Jax tries to sooth Kenzie's emotions.

Kenzie listens to Jax. She told herself a long time ago she would never let anyone see her cry, and she is not about to start now. "Fine, but remember, Ian, Connor is a little boy. Kayla is your age and able to handle herself. I'm sure of that," Kenzie tells Ian. "I've known this entire time we were trying to find a way to get Kayla back for you, but Connor was never part of the plan. Now he is, and it's not only my job, but yours as well to get him back."

"I know, Kenzie. I'm sorry I said those things to you. I know how those words made you feel, but I am truly sorry for them. It's my fault that Brayden and Connor were taken in the first place. I should have gone to Maria's room alone, before sending Brayden and Connor there. That is why your brother is not here with us now. It's because of me, and I'm sorry, Kenzie. Can you ever forgive me?" Ian pleads with Kenzie.

"No, I'm the one that should be sorry. I never knew you were holding all of that inside yourself. It's not your fault Connor is not here. It's Maria's fault, don't forget that" Kenzie reassures Ian.

"Um, I hate to break this up, but there is something I need to tell you about Maria," Jax speaks up.

"What do you have to tell us about Maria? The woman kidnapped Brayden and Connor and has taken them away from the school, and from me!" Kenzie exclaims, still a little upset about the conversation between her and Ian.

"Well, there is one last thing the Chancellor told me before I left."

"Stop rambling and get on it with already," Ian tells Jax

Jax snaps back to his current position, standing in front of two children that need him to be a leader right now, not some babbling older history teacher. "Sorry. The Chancellor told me that if Maria asks for my help, that I am to help her. I do not know what that means, but I have a feeling that she is telling me that Maria is to be trusted. I don't know how to describe it, but I think Maria is on our side. Therefore, Kenzie, you don't have to worry about Connor. He is in good hands with Brayden being with him, as he would not let anyone hurt him," Jax finishes the final piece of the puzzle he left out earlier.

"You have to be joking. You can't be serious that we are supposed to trust Maria now? All because someone you trust, but we don't know, tells us to help Maria when and if she asks for it? This is also coming from the same person who, like you said, has not only broken the rules of the Believers, but also the laws of your people. How can any of this even seem right to you? How can you fully trust Chancellor Billie June?" Ian questions everything Jax as just told them.

"I can fully trust Chancellor Billie June, since she told me these things she did, knowing they were rules and laws broken against our people, but she believed it to be the right thing to do. That to me makes her more of a Believer that anyone I know. Think about it, Ian. Chancellor Billie June risked and gave up everything she was raised to believe, to make sure that the other unknown, or unspoken, bloodline of Peter Hele had a part of their heritage. She made sure Sebastian's half-sister had a piece of the Time Keeper. If that sounds truly wrong and unforgivable, then you can go ahead and disbelieve the Chancellor. I, on the other hand, find what she did to be a selfless act to truly save the Hele bloodline and to make sure that eventually, they would find each other. Kind of like they have done now, with you and Kayla," Jax finishes.

"I understand what you are saying, Jax. Please understand, all of this is new to me," Ian confesses to Jax.

"I think what the Chancellor did was brave. Even in today's society, people don't seem to stand up for what they believe in when they believe it to be the right thing to do. They are afraid of what others will say, or think of them. Today's people seem to just follow along with the group like sheep. So, for the Chancellor to do something wrong, that she knew was the right thing to do, makes her very brave in my book," Kenzie expresses her opinion of the Chancellor. "I think you need to get a grip and start trusting people again, Ian."

"That's a lot easier said than done, Kenzie. People should earn someone's trust, not just expect it because of who they are. I didn't say what the Chancellor did was not the right thing to do, but her actions after what she did say a lot about her as well," Ian explains to Kenzie.

"I don't understand what you mean. She was removed as Sebastian's watcher. There was nothing she could have done to prevent that from happening, or was there? Jax?" Kenzie asks for clarification.

"No, Kenzie. There was nothing the Chancellor could have don't to change being removed as Sebastian's watcher, but that is not exactly what Ian is leading to. Ian, I will let you finish with what you were saying," Jax clears things up for Kenzie and allows Ian to get back to his story.

"Thank you, Jax. No, Kenzie, her removal as Sebastian's watcher was a consequence of her actions for not returning the Time Keeper in time for Sebastian to find it. The action I am referring to is her choice to stay silent about Camryn and there being another branch of the Hele family bloodline. That secret she kept to herself, until now, is the reason for my distrust in her. Why would she not tell the other Believers about Camryn, so they could create another set of Believers to watch her family bloodline? I feel that choice was a selfish one to make and left the other bloodline defenseless, if anyone else was to have found out about them, before now. Also, her choice of not telling anyone about Camryn, or her family, the knowledge of their heritage, or even the gifts the ring could possibly hold. Speaking of that, Jax, what can the ring do?" Ian finishes his reasoning on his trust issues.

"To be totally honest with you, Ian, I don't know what the ring can do, if anything. No one knows what the ring does, or what part of the Hele bloodline can access or use it, if it does have powers," Jax confesses.

"See, this is exactly what I am talking about. Because of the Chancellor's choice to remain silent about the ring and Sebastian's half-sister, now we are up against something we don't know anything about. It's a problem she helped create. The one thing we do know the ring can do is erase their bloodline from history, when it is near the Time Keeper. And the only person who can answer these questions is the person who erased themselves from the future," Ian states to Jax and Kenzie.

"Are you sure about that?" Kenzie speaks up.

"Excuse me? You don't think I know about my own best friend, who is now gone from history, who we have been trying to save and bring back to this timeline? I'm the only person who knew she existed in the beginning, so don't tell me I don't know what I'm talking about!" Ian exclaims.

"Sorry, Ian, that is not what I meant by that. What I am talking about is Junior. You say Junior can visit your dreams? Do you think it's because of the Time Keeper being part of the ring? If it is, do you think he can also access Kayla's dreams? I mean, since she is part of your family bloodline and has access to the Time Keeper with the ring?" Kenzie utilizes her Cooper education to narrow down the facts of Junior and the ring in general.

"I'm not sure. Junior only realized that Kayla erased herself from history. When it was too late for him to change anything, he vanished right in front of me. I'm not sure what Junior truly knows about his past or future family history. All I know is that he found out so late that his mother, Kayla, went back in history and erased herself from it, which in return caused a time ripple to catch up to him in the future, causing him to be erased as well," Ian answers.

"Let's say Junior doesn't remember his past, or his future or his mother, but what if you talk to him and explain all of this to him? Do you think he would be able to understand? I mean, you and Junior do share a connection for some reason, and if he's not your child, or a close relative, how else would he be able to contact you in your dreams? Why didn't he just go directly to his mother, Kayla's dreams?" Jax decided to question Ian, so he doesn't feel left out of an important conversation between the children.

"And what do you expect me to do? Do you think I can just think of Junior and he will appear? I have never been able to make contact with him. He has always made a connection with me. I would not know the first thing about trying to get in contact with Junior," Ian confesses to them both.

"How about this? You go to sleep like the last time you went to sleep, and Brayden and I tried to guide you to access the Time Keeper. Remember Junior intervened and kicked us out of your mind? What if you went to sleep and I tried to pull you somewhere else? Maybe to the Time Keeper, or to try to get you to think of where you saw Kayla in the mirror at the Bed, Bath, & Beyond? Do you think that could draw Junior's attention to you? Maybe even enough for him to kick me out of your mind? Then when he shows up, you can make sure he doesn't kick me out, and we can both speak to him in your dream. We can explain what is going on and get him to go to Kayla's dreams and help us find out where they are," Kenzie is using her Cooper ISD education in overtime now.

"Wow, Kenzie. The way you think outside the box is extraordinary. What do you think, Ian? Do you think something like that could work?" Jax speaks with surprise.

"I'm not sure of anything anymore, but I don't see why we don't give it a try. What do you guys say? Should we try it?" Ian asks Jax and Kenzie.

"YES!" Kenzie shouts out at Ian and Jax.

"It's a yes from me as well," Jax agrees.

"Well, I don't think we have time to go to one of our rooms. So, I will lie down here on this couch and force myself to fall asleep. Once I'm asleep, I'll focus on the image of Kayla in the mirror from the store as Kenzie suggested. When I am asleep, Kenzie, feel free to jump in at any time. Maybe you can help me stay focused on Kayla and make sure I don't venture off inside my own mind. Once Junior, if he comes, is there, you can try to stay, and we can explain things to him together, like you said before. Unless he kicks you out before we get the chance to stop him. If he does, then don't try to come back in. I'm pretty sure doing that may cause him to get upset and possibly leave," Ian spouts out instructions.

"I can handle that," Kenzie retorts back to Ian.

"And just what do you suggest that I do?" Jax asks, feeling left out again.

"We will need you to stand guard. There are so many points of entry into this room, we need you to make sure we stay safe. Once Kenzie has been, if she is, kicked out of my mind by Junior, she can help you keep guard. But until then, you are our only defense. We are putting our lives and trust in your hands. Please don't let us down, Jax," Ian pleads with him.

"I won't let either of you down. You both are safe with me here."

Before Ian could say anything to Jax, he has already turned his back to Ian and Kenzie, in order for him to begin his guard duties.

Now with Jax on guard, Ian takes his place lying down on the couch he has been sitting on in the Sky Lounge of the school. As he falls softly back on to the pillow pressed against the arm of the couch, for his head to rest on, Kenzie is making herself a spot on the floor, next to Ian on the couch.

As Ian drifts off to dreamland, Kenzie waits for her opportunity to join him. After about twenty minutes, Kenzie makes her move to join Ian in his dreams. As Kenzie eases into Ian's mind, she finds herself in a memory of Ian at a restaurant in Atlanta called 'Bada Bings.' He's there paying trivia with his mom and dad on a Friday night, while they are on vacation. The place is so crowded, but Ian feels at ease because of the people working there. Jorden, Maryanne, Chad, Doug, Sara, David, and Kaylee make everyone feel so comfortable as soon as they walk in. He hopes that his social phobia stays at bay, and he will be enjoying his time here.

Kenzie walks up to Ian's table once their servicer leaves with their order. "Ian? Hey, it's me, Kenzie. Do you remember me?"

"Oh, hey, Kenzie. What are you doing here? Are you on vacation with your family too?"

"I came here to see you. Can we go into the game room to talk for just a few minutes? I promise I'll bring you right back."

"Mom, Dad, I am going to talk to my friend Kenzie for a few minutes. Is that okay?"

As Ian's parents agree to let him go with Kenzie to the game room of the restaurant, Kenzie pulls Ian back to the sports room with the pool tables and shuffleboard, so she can talk to him.

"Ian, please understand what I am about to tell you. I am here to make you focus on Kayla. I'm here to make sure you know this is a dream, and we are really here because we need to find Kayla. Do you understand?" Kenzie asks Ian inside his dream.

"I'm sorry, but what are you talking about? Who is Kayla?" Ian replies to Kenzie.

When Ian says those words, 'Who is Kayla,' Junior joins them.

"What do you mean, who's Kayla?" Junior asks Ian.

"Who are you, and why are you asking me that?" Ian spits back at Junior.

"It's me, Junior. Don't you know who I am at least?"

"What is happening to me right now? I'm just here to eat and play trivia with my parents while we are on vacation. But now everything is starting to get weird."

Before Ian can complete his mental breakdown, Kenzie has pulled her arm back, and is now swinging it directly at Ian's face with an open palm. 'SLAP' is all you can hear in the game room in the back of 'Bada Binds of Atlanta.'

"Ouch, Kenzie! Why are you slapping me? And Junior, when did you get here?"

"Finally, you are here with us," Kenzie expresses her relief.

"And why are you here? I told you that I can take care of Ian. I think it's time you left us for now," Junior tells Kenzie.

Before Junior has a chance to remove Kenzie from Ian's dream, Ian speaks up, "No! Stop! Please, let Kenzie stay this time. This is actually her idea for us to get in contact with you. I beg you to please let Kenzie stay, so she can help me explain to you why we are here now and what we need to tell you," Ian pleads with Junior.

"Are you saying you called me here? How is that even possible? I am hardly able to control my powers to even find your dreams. How did she know this would work? And what do you have to tell me that you think I don't already know? I'm from the future, remember?" Junior questions both Ian and Kenzie's motives.

"Junior, we don't have much time to fill you in, but with Kenzie's gifts, she will be able to fill you in much faster. Right now, time is not on our side. With or without the Time Keeper, we need your help. You are the only one that can help put history back on track. That means saving your mother, Kayla," Ian lets Junior realize the severity of the situation.

"Okay, Ian. I trust you. Kenzie can stay, and you both can fill me in on what is going on," Junior concedes.

And with that invitation, Ian and Kenzie begin to fill Junior in on everything. They tell him how Kayla is missing, and there is a mysterious person from the future that takes control of other people's bodies from this time, but in a way is helping them. Then Kenzie uses her gifts to connect with Junior's mind to show him the mirror from the store that she could not see Kayla in, but Ian did. She was able to show Junior what Ian saw, because Ian had shown her the exact image before starting this quest. While Kenzie is connected to Junior, she expresses how important it is that he finds Kayla, in her dreams. They want him to do it the same way he did with Ian's dreams. They need him to find out where Kayla is being held and to let her know that they are coming there for her and the others.

"How do you even think I can do that? I don't know my mother as a child. I was only able to find you, Ian, because of the stories my mother told me about you," Junior tells Ian.

"Good, think back to those memories about me. Now, did she ever tell you any stories about both of us, like anything we used to do, or places we would go?"

"You mean, like the time you both watched a scary movie after my grandparents went to bed, and you were both so scared, you had to sleep in the same room for a week? A story like that one?" Junior actually cracks a small smile.

"Is that the only story she told you about us?"

"No, but I thought it was funny enough to tell out loud. So, yes, I have other stories of you both, but when I was told these stories, I was a child. I was only paying attention to you in the stories," Junior confesses sadly.

"What if I repeat some of the stories, the ones she told you, and I will focus on her this time? Do you want to give that a try? Kenzie can help you with visions of how she looks in this time period. So? What do you say?"

"You know we are going to have to do this in here, inside your mind, right?" Junior tells Ian.

"Yes, which actually just may help us. Now start telling me what stories she told you."

Junior begins to tell Ian some of the stories Kayla has told him over the years about her and Ian's childhood. Once he would mention an event, Ian would tell the story, but this time focusing on Kayla. As Ian describes the story, Kenzie pulls out the vision in Ian's mind of that story and places it into Junior's mind. After the initial shock of having Kenzie put a vision in his mind passes, the rest of the visions placed by Kenzie feel natural to Junior. They continue with this method, until all of a sudden, Junior vanishes from Ian's dream.

"What happened? What did you do, Kenzie?"

"I didn't do anything, except place your memories inside his mind of the events you were telling him. Second, what makes you think I would have done something?"

"Junior? Are you still here?" Ian shouts inside his dream.

"I don't think he is here, Ian. Do you think he was able to feel Kayla in her dreams with all the information you gave him?"

"Well, if he's not here, let's hope it worked. Now, wake up and then wake me up, so we can tell Jax."

Kenzie snaps out of Ian's mind, half scaring Jax, who let out a low scream. Then she leans over and gently wakes Ian. Ian begins to wipe his eyes and sits up on the couch he has been lying on.

"Jax, we need to talk. You will never believe what just happened to us. We were able to get Junior here, but then..."

Chapter 16

Kenzie's Plan?

As Brayden gets comfortable on the bed in the room next to Kayla's, the others find places to make their own as well. They have no idea how long they are going to be here, or how long this is going to take, if it works at all.

This is going to be a long night, Maria thinks to herself.

Kayla has already fallen fast asleep, due to the long day she has had, part of it with Mason, and the other part with Garrett. Part of herself wishes she would have taken a nap, as she suggested to Mason. That did not matter to her now, as Kayla was deep in her dreams.

"So, Brayden. What do you need in order to break into Kayla's dreams?" Mason asks.

"Nothing at the moment. All I have to do is focus on Kayla's energy, then I can slip right in. I don't have to be asleep to do this either, but this bed is pretty comfortable," Brayden tells Mason.

"I thought you said they were ready to cooperate with us. This smart mouth does not sound like cooperation to me," Mason says as he looks over at Maria, Garrett, Connor, and Maclaine.

"Oh, he is ready. Brayden is just a bit of a class clown. He means nothing by his words. Right, Brayden?" Maria replies to Mason, while giving Brayden a stare that would scare a scarecrow.

"Yes, ma'am. I'm ready to get this started, that's all. I will keep my jokes to the very minimum, Mr. Mason, sir," Brayden speaks to them both, Mason and Maria. "I will go ahead now and try to make a connection with Kayla."

Waiting for no replies or instructions, Brayden closes his eyes and begins to feel for Kayla's energy with his thoughts. Being as close as they are to each other, it does not take Brayden long to find Kayla's energy. Now that he has located her, Brayden slowly begins to enter Kayla's mind with his. This is when Brayden begins to cover his ears as he is lying on the bed in the room for all to see.

"What is he doing right now?" Mason asks Maria.

"How would I know? I've never seen him do this before," Maria replies. "Maybe we should pull Brayden out for now and find out what is going on."

"We will do no such thing. We are going to let this play out, no matter the outcome," Mason responds with a very cold heart.

"There is so much music in Kayla's head. All I can hear is Kelly Clarkson's song, 'Piece by Piece,' blaring in her mind, over and over again. I'm not sure what is going on here, but it's so loud. I don't know how she is even able to sleep through this music. This would normally wake someone up. It's as if she can't hear it, but only I can," Brayden speaks out loud, while lying on the bed as he is breaking off his connection with Kayla. Then he sits up on the bed, still covering his ears as if he can still hear the music that was playing.

"Why did you stop? I don't remember telling you that you get to make any decisions on what happens in here," Mason says, upset with Brayden.

"I stopped because if I were to stay in her mind, or as close to her mind as I could get, I would be dead. That music is a defense spell that has been placed on her mind for some reason. Put there by someone who knows what they are doing, I might add," Brayden corrects Mason.

"Well, when can we go back in, or at least try again?" Mason asks Brayden.

"Just give me a little time and I will try again. I'm going to need all my strength if I want to break past that barrier of Kelly Clarkson," Brayden replies. "That girl can sing!"

"Fine, you have thirty minutes, and then you will try again," Mason directs Brayden.

***

"Mom? Is this where I am? Am I in your dreams?" Junior asks as he finds himself in a place away from Ian and Kenzie. He knows he is no longer in the game room at Bada Bings. "Mom?"

There is no response to Junior's questions. He is so confused right now. He is not sure what to do, or where he is. Then he thinks of another way to get her attention. "Kayla? Are you here?"

"Who is talking to me?" Kayla replies.

"Is this really you? I can't believe that I'm actually here and that Ian and Kenzie's idea really worked," Junior says to Kayla with excitement.

"Did you say Ian? How do you know Ian? And who is Kenzie? I've never heard Ian talk about anyone named Kenzie before."

"Yes, I said Ian. Your best friend, Ian. Both, one in the same. Kenzie is a friend of Ian's from his new school."

"Then who are you? And why would Ian send you to me, if that's what you are leading to?"

"Oh, I'm sorry. My name is Junior and I'm… a friend of Ian's too, from school. That's why you don't know me. And they, Ian and Kenzie, asked me to help them get a message to you, even though they don't know where you are. They want me to tell you they are coming to find you and break you out of…"

"This compound? Is that the word you are looking for? The reason I ask is because that is what I am stuck in. I'm being held in a compound."

"Okay, a compound. Where is this compound that you speak of located? This will make things easier for them to come get you, knowing the exact location of where you are."

"Do you think I have any clue as to even what state I am in, much less where I am right now? I went to sleep in Brooklynn, I think, and I woke up here. I do not remember being transported here, so I don't know where I am. How do you expect me to tell you where I am?"

"I'm not too sure, I guess. I was not prepared for this. I think Ian and Kenzie expected you to know where you are. I don't think they took in to account that you may have been asleep, or just not know where you are."

"So? What do we do now? Sit and wait for them to come somewhere that I don't even know the location of?"

"What's that loud music? Do you hear it?"

"I do, and I love that song. That's 'Piece by Piece' by the one and only Kelly Clarkson. I don't know why it is so loud in my head right now, because I haven't heard this song is some time now. Do you feel that?"

"Feel what? All I can feel is the beat of the song. Is that what you are referring to?"

"No. It feels like I'm being pushed back into my dream for some reason. I don't think I can resist it, Junior. I think this may be part of Alexis's defenses to protect my mind. Tell Ian that I'm sorry that I don't know where I am, but I have to go and I think you should go as well," Kayla expresses to Junior as she disappears into her dreams again.

Before Junior has a chance to go after Kayla, or even say anything to her, the next thing he notices is that he is standing back in front of Ian and Kenzie, in Ian's mind.

"What just happened?" Junior asks either of the two.

"It worked! I told you that it would work," Kenzie shouts to Ian.

"Kenzie, what worked?" Junior asks.

"You know my name? Please, don't kick me out of Ian's mind. I can help Ian describe things to you…"

"Yes, by showing me the vision of them from Ian's mind and placing them into mine. We have already been over this, that is why I am back," Junior finishes Kenzie's explanation.

"You mean we have already called you here, explained the plan for you to find Kayla, and you have already done that?" Ian asks in shock.

"Yes. Then as you were still explaining the stories of you and my mom, the next thing I know is that I was in my mom's mind. I tried to call for her, but she didn't reply to my calls, so I asked if Kayla was here instead of 'Mom,' and she answered back. We didn't get to talk long because of the music, but I did get to tell mom, Kayla, that you sent me to her dreams to try and see if she could tell me where she was. But she said she woke up wherever she is, and doesn't know where that is. In other words, she has no clue where she is. Then the music got so loud, she said she was being pushed back into her dream. Kayla told me to tell you, Ian that she is sorry that she doesn't know where she is. Next thing I know, she is gone, and I am here with you two, again, acting all weird for some reason," Junior explains to Kenzie and Ian, hoping it will clear up their memory.

After Junior finished, Ian and Kenzie are both silent. Junior is unsure if it's because they found out he has already seen them and carried out their task, or because Kayla does not know where she is being held. Junior himself is not sure why he went back a short moment in time, but time travel is nothing new to him anymore.

"So, what you are telling us is that our plan won't, or didn't give us the answers that we need?" Ian speaks finally. "You were our only option. If that doesn't work, then I don't know what we can do. Do either of you have any suggestions?"

"I'm not sure if I can be of any more help for you right now. I may be able to get into my mother's mind, but we already know that's not helpful. Why don't you both wake up, so you can think with a mind that is not swimming in dream world? And don't worry about me, you know I won't be far away," Junior suggests to Ian and Kenzie.

"If you think it's the best thing for us right now, then I guess it won't hurt anything by thinking of something else. Thank you Junior for almost, or actually completing the task," Ian turns and gives

Kenzie a nod to go ahead and break her connection, so he can wake up.

Kenzie comes to as she leaves Ian's mind, and Ian wakes up just as quickly as Kenzie does. Once they are both awake, they look at each other, then realize that Jax is standing over them, staring at them both.

"Well? Where you able to find out what happened to Junior?" Jax asks.

"How do you know about something going on with Junior?" Ian asks Jax.

"Because you both told me that you were able to reach Junior, but before you were able to tell everything, he disappeared. That's when you both woke up and told me. Then about ten minutes ago, you went back to sleep to try to call him back again. Don't you remember any of this?"

"No, because this is our first time trying to call for Junior, and talking to him and waking up. But Junior seemed to think that we had already talked to him, so he cut us off and explained how the mission went in Kayla's dream," Kenzie answers Jax this time.

"Let me get this straight. Apparently, when you went to sleep the second time, you actually went back to the first time, before seeing Junior?"

"It would seem so. But why? How long ago was it when we woke up the first time?" Ian questions Jax.

"Let's see now, I would say you both woke up about forty-five minutes ago, but went back to sleep only ten minutes ago."

"So, Kenzie and I have forty-five minutes of time reset. But why? We did not learn anything from Junior, and how did we reset to forty-five minutes before calling for Junior? There has to be a reason for this extra time. Now, we just need to figure out what we can do different, while we have the time," Ian expresses out loud.

"Do you think it's just us, or do you think anyone in Kayla's group has also gained forty-five minutes?" Kenzie inquires.

"I guess we will have to wait and see. But right now, we need to focus on what to do next," Ian suggests.

***

"Where am I?"

"Who said that? Is someone else inside my mind?"

"I guess I am in your mind, but I don't see anything. It's all dark. I can somehow access your mind, but I'm unable to see any more about you. Normally when I enter someone's mind, I have access to all of their thoughts and memories, but with you I do not have access to anything. I am unable to see your thoughts or dreams. This has never happened to me before. Who are you?"

"Well, I can tell you this, no one should be able to penetrate my mind, and I can't feel a body for your energy source. Why is that?"

"Why are you asking so many questions when I have just as many for you? Can we at least start with names? My name is Junior. What's yours?"

"You're right. We could go back and forth all night with questions neither of us would answer. Well, Junior, my name is Garrett. It's nice to meet you."

"Nice to meet you too. It's funny that your name is Garrett, because that's my real name too. I just go by Junior, because I am a Jr."

"That's cool. So, when you enter people's minds, you can usually see things? What kind of things?"

"Well, I can only enter someone's mind while they are asleep, so I can see their dreams. Then once I'm in, I can show certain people other things. That's why I find it odd that I'm here and can't see your dreams."

"I can answer that for you. It's because I am not asleep right now, I am wide awake. You are talking to me in my mind in its awakened state, and I am thinking my questions and answers to you. I can't let anyone hear what's going on right now. This is pretty bad timing, if there ever was such a thing. Right now I am sitting, waiting for a friend to wake up and possibly lie and get caught, or be good enough to be able to give us more time with our mission."

"What do you mean you are awake? I've never been able to enter a mind that was not asleep. And why is this a bad time?"

"For some reason I feel you may understand, so I'll tell you. I'm in a room watching a friend use his powers to try and dream walk another friend, Kayla, in another room, but it doesn't look like it's going too well. He just keeps repeating, 'Piece by Piece' by Kelly Clarkson, it's so loud. We have no idea what that means yet, because he has not woken up and is still trying to dream walk her."

"Did you just say Kayla? And your friend is in her mind, but only hears 'Piece by Piece' by Kelly Clarkson?"

"Yes, why do you ask?"

"Because I was just in a person named Kayla's mind and that song started playing so loud that I got kicked out of her mind and sent back to Ian's."

"Did you say Ian's mind?" Garrett blinks, but hopes no one noticed his attention being split two ways.

"Yes, and Kenzie was there too. But they somehow went back in time, or I did, because when I went back to them, they didn't remember our earlier meeting, or sending me to Kayla's mind in the first place. They tried to repeat the entire thing over again, but I cut them off. I told them she was not able to tell me where she was being held. They are trying to find out where she is being held, so they can come and rescue her and the other two that were kidnapped by Maria, I think."

"Today is your lucky day, because I can help you with that."

Epilogue: High Court

The two days have already come and gone, and the remaining leaders have only been able to test a few theories. A couple of them seem very promising to the Council and become the High Court.

"Let me just say that the little progress we have made in the past week has been pretty good, but we have to do better. These little things we have accomplished will only work if they can use them properly," the Council leader speaks to the High Court, Fisher, Payton, and Emma.

"I have to agree. With my people being able to place the puzzle piece for Kayla to find, we still need a way to show her what to do with it to make it work," Fisher of the Aquarians admits.

"Well, let me tell you this, going back in time to give someone an extra forty-five minutes just to figure out a new plan is not easy. Giving time to someone, while already in time travel mode takes a lot out of us," Emma of the Fairley Folk expresses. "They will have to use that time wisely, because we cannot go back and tell them what to do with it."

"Why are all of you complaining? I've had to do what I can on my own. It seems that just because my brother vanished, it doesn't mean the hate of our people towards him did as well. They hate me as if I'm

Preston, so I have had no help from my people. With that being said, I think what I have been able to do will work," King Payton of the Embers informs the High Court.

"And what is it that you did that you think is so amazing that it will solve all of our problems and concerns?" Fisher asks.

"Why don't you allow him to finish with what he is saying, if you want to know?" Rose is asking Fisher, defending King Payton.

"Thank you, Rose, but I can defend and answer for myself, if you don't mind. I mean no disrespect to you, please know that. Now, what I was in the middle of saying is that I was able to get Junior to connect with Garrett's mind."

"And what is so special about that? He has been able to go in and out of others' minds ever since he went back in time," Emma asks.

"I was able to do it while Garrett was awake. And to top it off, neither of them even know who the other is. Its genius if I do say so myself," King Payton tells the High Court.

"Or the worst thing you could have done. Did you even think about the consequences of if they DO find out who they are? That alone can change history in the most severe way possible. In a way, that could make all of us to be removed from the present. You need to figure out a way to make this work before you end us all," the Council leader demands of King Payton.

Everyone is in such shock as to what King Payton has done, that they can't bear to even look at him, much less speak to him. Everyone is whispering to each other around the table, leaving King Payton out of their conversations.

"This is going to work. The reason it will work is because of the things you have done before me. The puzzle piece you left for her, Fisher, and the extra forty-five minutes you gave her, Emma. Those things are the most important things I needed to make my plan work. I thought this was a group effort. For people that only want to help get history back on track, you are very quick to judge another's motives or plans. I did not question any of your methods, so I would expect the same about mine from you," King Payton says as he begins to walk out of the Council meeting room. "I guess only time will tell if I am right, or if you are, but if you are, then none of this even matters, does it?"

Acknowledgements

I would like to thank Jorden and the entire team at Bada Bings Atlanta, for allowing me to call their amazing sports bar my office during a time of need. They are truly amazing people, being new to Atlanta, I needed a place where I could feel comfortable enough to sit and write. This was that place for me. I also would like to thank my family, as always, for being my biggest supporters and fans. Not to mention, characters.

Next, I would like to thank my editor, Patricia, of Carpenter Editing Services, LLC. She has been a second mother to me for many years and with her editing skills, advice, and opinions on *Time Keeper, School Bound, Search Begins, and now Loose Ends*. Without her, this work of art would not be what it is today. She brings such joy in my writing with her suggestions and honest critiques. Not to mention, her patience with me has been amazing. With my reading disability, she has been able to teach me more about proper English and being able to become a better writer. Along with my Editor, I need to thank my Beta Reader, Jordan Eagles, whose feedback was amazing and helped create this final product. Now, I have one more Beta Reader I would like to give thanks to, and that would Bernadette Horgan. You can follow her on Instagram

@bibliophile1996, if you want to send her something to read and leave amazing reviews for you. Thank you all.

I would also like to give a quick thank you to the places that allowed me to sit and write in their establishments when I needed that creative energy. A few of those places are Overtime Grill and Bar (off Lakeshore Pkwy in Birmingham, AL), Dunkin Donuts (off HWY 119 in Pelham, AL), Tejano's Tex-Mex (Cooper, TX), Bada Bing's Atlanta (Atlanta, GA), Pencil Factory Shops & Flats (Atlanta, GA), DoubleTree Hotel (Chattanooga Downtown, TN), Blakes (Atlanta, GA), Friends on Ponce (Atlanta, GA), and Barns & Noble Edgewood (Atlanta, GA). Without these places listed I would have been lost, as someone with ASD, social settings are not easy for me, and I never felt out of place or any pressure at these creative energy spots. These places made me feel at home every time.

Last, but not least, my fans. If not for you, my words would sit on paper, never to be read.

Continue along with Ian on his final journey, as he continues to find a way to save his best friend, Kayla, in *Final Hour*.

An Exciting and Adventurous way to view History

Book Five of the

Saving History Series

Final

Hour

Robert Starnes

Prologue: Travis the Fixer?

"And just where do you think you are going? You cannot create the greatest possible mess in history, then just walk out and leave the rest of us to wait to see if what you have done was the right, or wrong thing to do," the Council leader billowed to King Payton, before he walks completely out of the Council meeting room.

"Do not think that just because my brother is gone that you can speak to me in any way you want. It would serve you to remember that I am a King. Not just any King, but the King of the Embers. So, if you enjoy our world as it is now, then back off," King Payton demands.

With those final words from the King, the remaining High Leaders, Fisher and Emma, along with the Council leader allowed King Payton to leave the room. The room remained silent, until Travis of the Windairians walks back into the meeting room. As he enters, all heads turn in disbelief. They all know that Travis was excused from the group for not being able to help out with time travel. Obviously, that was not the truth, or they would not be back here now. They can help with time travel.

Travis walks into the room, walks directly over to his spot he once occupied at the Council table, and takes a seat. "What's the matter with you all? You act as if you are seeing a ghost."

"I'm sorry, Travis, but you have already claimed that you have no idea of what we actually need from your people, and because of that you have been dismissed. This is not the type of meeting where you can just come back when you want to. Our circumstances have not changed; therefore, you are still not needed, unless your abilities have changed. Have they?" the Council leader asks Travis bluntly.

"You might say that they have. Let's say that we, with my help, are going to be able to help some of the things you all messed up in the past so far. Trust me when I say you are going to need our help before this is even close to being corrected," Travis defines his current abilities.

About the time Travis finishes, King Payton walks back into the Council meeting room. "What's he doing here?" he asks while pointing at Travis.

"Claiming he can fix what we have done to the past, but we are all assuming he is talking about what you have done most of all," Rose explains to King Payton.

"How dare you speak to me in that way…"

"I'm sorry to cut you off, King Payton, but we don't have any time for your threats of 'how dare you' right now. If you could please take your seat and let me get started, I will show you all what you all have done wrong," Travis instructs the King, as he follows his instruction and takes his seat.

"Now, can I begin?" Travis asks the group.

Chapter 1

Garrett's Mind

"And how can you help me? Do you know the location of Kayla, Brayden, Connor, and Maria?" Junior asks Garrett's mind he's now in.

"Actually, I do. I know because I am here with them all. I have been with your two friends since they arrived, and I can assure you they have not been harmed," Garrett replies to Junior.

"Great, then where are you so I can tell Ian and Kenzie. That way they can come there, where you are now, and help you rescue all of them, except Maria that is," Junior demands.

"Wait a second there, Junior. I can't tell you where we are right now, because it will put all of us in danger. We have to let Brayden continue trying to get into Kayla's mind. Brayden will be able to lie to Mason about what he sees, but this swill be the only way to get Mason to stop trying this and to start trusting Kayla more. Do you understand?" Garrett asks Junior.

"Not in the least. I don't know why it is so important for Mason to trust Kayla, when Ian and his friends are willing to come and rescue them all, including Kayla," Junior spits back to Garrett.

"Junior, there is more riding on this mission than just a rescue. History is at stake here. You can't come and just save everyone, we have to make a difference. If Ian and Kenzie come and just save everyone, then this will be the history that remains. And it will be repeated again and again, unless we change Mason's outlook on life, or just in general. Now do you understand how important this mission is, for the future?" Garrett pleads with Junior.

"How do you know so much about the future? Are you from the future?" Junior asks Garrett.

"I don't see how any of that information can help us now, do you? Speaking of the future, why is it that I can't feel a body attached to your mind?" Garrett digs deeper with Junior.

"Excuse me? You said that before. How can you tell if I have a body or not? I can promise you that I most certainly do have a body!"

"Let's say I have special gifts like the others here, and this is one of mine. Now, you say you have a body, but it can't be in this time period; therefore, you are from the future or the past. Which now leads me to some questions, like what are you doing here now? Also, what do you hope to change, and who are you going to have to use to achieve your goals?"

"I'm sorry, but we do not have time for such questions. I am somehow here, in your mind, while you are awake, that has to mean something. You know your location and I need it, so you can at least give me your location. If you think I should wait before telling Ian and Kenzie, then I will wait, but at least tell me. This way, if anything happens to you, I will be able to tell the others where you are, before anyone else gets hurt."

"As long as you don't divulge our location until I tell you, then it's okay. Do you understand what I am saying, and do you agree?"

"Yes, I understand and promise to follow your instructions."

"Then I will show you our location, but I can't stress enough how important it is that you wait until I tell you it's okay to hurry up and get here. Please, you have to understand that. All of our future lives depend on you waiting to tell Ian and the others."

"Yes, I said that I promise. I will not give anyone your location, until you tell me it's all right. Now that I have been inside your mind, if you need me, all you have to do is think of me when you need my help. I will feel that and will be able to come back anytime I'm needed."

With that, Garrett shows their location with Junior's mind, but as soon as he does, he has to ask Junior to leave, because Mason is not happy with the outcome from Brayden's work. "Junior, I'm sorry but it's time you left. Mason is not very happy right now and wants all of our full attention. Please, go back to Ian and Kayla and let them know that everything is fine for now. But if things get bad, you will be able to lead them here, and only then. Understand?"

"Yes, Garrett, I completely understand, and I will not say anything about your location, unless you ask me," are the last words Junior says to Garrett before he is removed from Garrett's mind.

***

As Garrett has lost the connection with Junior with his mind, he is able to listen to what Mason is talking about. He is apparently upset that Brayden has been unable to penetrate Kayla's mind. Brayden has been unable to dream walk Kayla, because of a Kelly song, 'Broken Pieces,' which kept playing extremely loud in Kayla's mind. This caused Brayden to not be able to actually enter Kayla's mind. All Brayden could hear was the song repeating, over and over again in Kayla's mind without being able to go any further into Kayla's memories. They are calling it some kind of defense spell that was put in Kayla's mind by someone else.

"Well, Mason, who could have put such a strange defense spell on Kayla's mind?" Maria asks.

"There is only one person I can think of, but if it is true, then that means we have a lot more problems to worry about than just Kayla's mind being blocked," Mason responds.

"What do you mean? And who do you think it could be that has placed this block on her mind?" Maria questions Mason.

"That is not a topic we should get into right now. Right now, we need Brayden to try again to dream walk Kayla," Mason explains. "Are you able and ready to try again to dream walk Kayla?" Mason asks Brayden.

"Yes, I can try again. Now that I know what I am up against, I may be able to force myself past that barrier. Let's just hope that this is the only barrier that has been placed on Kayla's mind, or this could be a very long process," Brayden informs the room.

"Then it's time to lie back down and face the music. Do you think you can handle her music?" Mason asks somewhat jokingly.

"We are about to find out," Brayden answers, while lying back on the bed again. As Brayden closes his eyes and begins to breach Kayla's mind, so he can try and dream walk her again, he is met with the song again, 'Broken Pieces,' blearing in Kayla's mind.

Brayden decides to take a different approach this time. Brayden begins to sing along with the song in a very loud voice. To his surprise, The song stops playing in Kayla's mind. Now Brayden is able to move past the exterior of Kayla's mind.

Brayden takes this opportunity to go deeper into Kayla's mind to see what she is dreaming about. He knows it may be something he will have to lie about to Mason, but he also knows he has to go into Kayla's dreams at one point or another.

As Brayden moves deeper into Kayla's mind, the clearer things become. Now what he sees is not exactly what he is expecting. Brayden is able to see a small girl in the middle of a room, and he believes it to be Kayla. She is sitting in the middle of a room filled with puzzle pieces. She is not working on any puzzle, that Brayden can tell, she is just sitting in the middle of a room of puzzle pieces.

"Kayla? Do you remember me? Do you know who I am? It's me, Brayden, a friend of Ian's. I am here because Mason is expecting me to go back and tell him any secrets you may be hiding from him, but you don't have to worry about that. I am not going to tell Mason anything that he wants to know, but what we want him to think you know. Can you turn around and talk to me, Kayla?" Brayden asks the little girl sitting in the middle of the room of puzzle pieces who has her back turned to him.

Brayden begins to move closer to the little girl, but before he is able to make it to her, she turns around and tells him to stop.

"Please, don't come any closer to me. You are stepping on all the pieces and if you damage them, they won't be able to be put back together in the future. Is that why you are here? Has my father sent you here to make sure I stay broken forever?" the young girl asks the stranger to her, Brayden.

"I'm sorry. I thought you were a friend of mine, Kayla. But I can see that you aren't, so what's your name? My name is Brayden, and no, your father did not send me here. I was only sent here to find my friend, Kayla. I would never come here to try to make someone stay broken forever. I would actually want to help. Is there anything I can do for you to help you, while I look for my friend? I would hate to know that you are out here, somewhere, feeling like you are broken, because I can assure you, you are not broken. You are a special piece of a puzzle that is just waiting for the perfect puzzle to fit in for the rest of your life. I promise."

"Well, Brayden, my name is Kelly, and I don't know your friend, Kayla. I do know that if you don't stop moving around, you will destroy my chances of ever being put back together. I am supposed to be put back together, Broken Pieces, by someone who will restore my faith that a man can be kind and a father can stay. So, please stop destroying my chances of happiness," Kelly tells Brayden.

Kelly is sitting in a room full of puzzle pieces and the song that was playing was 'Broken Pieces' by an American singer. *What are the chances that this is a young that young singer, and this is another block in Kayla's mind?* Brayden wonders to himself.

"Where are we, Kelly? And what's your last name?" Brayden asks of Kelly.

"I'm not sure where we are. I have been here for so long, waiting to be who I am meant to be. And my full name is just Kelly. Why do you want to know?"

"I am just wanting to get a full grasp of where I am and whose mind I may be in. Are we in your mind, or are you a memory put inside of Kayla's mind?"

"I'm sorry, but I don't know what you're talking about. I'm going to have to ask you to leave my room now, so I can wait for HIM to show up and put me back together, because of all of the 'Broken Pieces' HE has left. So, if you don't mind, this is goodbye," Kelly tells Brayden and as she does, he is pulled out of Kelly's room and all the way back out to the sound of the song 'Broken Pieces' by the one and only little girl he just left, Kelly. The song is still so loud he breaks his connection with Kayla and wakes up in the bed in the room next to Kayla's room.

"What's wrong now, Brayden?" Mason asks.

"I think it is another block in Kayla's mind. I made it past the music barrier that was playing so loud, but this time I was transported to a room with a small girl in it. I assumed it was Kayla at first, but then I was corrected. The room I was in was full of puzzle pieces, and the small girl was sitting in the middle of the room. As I moved closer to her, after she did not answer my questions of who she was, she turned and stopped me from moving forward. She said I was damaging the puzzle pieces, and that someone is supposed to find them to put them back together. Then when I asked her what her name was, she said, 'Kelly.' I was seeing the inspiration behind the song that was playing in the outer part of the barrier, 'Broken Pieces' by the adult version of Kelly. I could feel the pain she was feeling as she was writing the words and singing them for their first time. I could feel her sorrow as I stood in the room with all the puzzle pieces just waiting to be found and put back together, so she could feel whole and loved again. Then she made me leave, and I ended up back in the part of Kayla's mind that actually was playing the song 'Broken Pieces' so loud that I had to break my connection with Kayla's mind," Brayden finishes.

"So, what you are telling us is that you still have not been able to dream walk Kayla?" Mason states to Brayden.

"No, what I am telling you is that there are several levels of protection around Kayla's mind. After the music, which I was able to get past, is another layer of protection. It's actually a room with a young Kelly sitting on the floor of a room full of puzzle pieces, but now I have to figure out how to pass this one. I am not going to be able to crack through, however many blocks she has in her mind tonight. I can assure you that. Those spells are strong, and each one requires more of my energy, which I am running low on right now," Brayden replies back to Mason.

As Brayden finishes, Mason begins to pace the floor of the bedroom they have been using. He is not saying a word, but he has a look of distrust on his face. Maria is not sure if Brayden is telling the truth or not, and that has her very worried.

"Is there anything you are leaving out? Something you don't want to tell me?" Mason finally speaks, breaking the silence to ask Brayden a few follow up questions.

"I have left nothing out. Everything I know about the inside of Kayla's mind, you know as well. Why would I want to hold anything from you? The sooner I do this for you, the sooner Connor and I can leave this place. So, trust me when I say, you will know what I know when I know it. And if I thought I could finish it right now, I would do it, so we could leave. The last thing I want is for Connor or I have to stay here any longer than we have to," Brayden snaps back to Mason.

If Mason had doubts before about Brayden's loyalties, they are all gone now. Mason has never had someone speak to him in that tone before, but he decides to let the matter pass, because he still needs Brayden. "Fine. Why don't we call it a night for their first try then? Garrett, Maclaine, will you two escort our guests down to their quarters in the basement cells, so they can get plenty of rest without being disturbed. Maria, you are welcome to use this room if you like. I am going to head to my office for a little bit of work before bed, then tomorrow evening we will start right back up where we left off, right here in this room. Is that understood?" Mason asks everyone.

With a quick nod from everyone, they all go their separate ways for the evening.

***

"You can come out now Kayla, he's gone."

"Are you sure he's gone?"

"Yes, I'm sure. Now come out here."

Kayla comes sneaking out from behind a piece of white wall that is undetectable by the naked eye. She makes her way over to Kelly, who is still sitting on the floor.

"I don't know how I can ever thank you enough for helping me. To be honest, I'm still not sure why you agreed to do this in the first place," Kayla comments to Kelly.

"Let's say that I owe a debt to Alexis, and she told me that one day she would ask for my help, and me helping her in the future is all she wanted for helping me at my present time. Plus, it was kind of fun playing a creepy little me, sitting in a room full of puzzle pieces," Kelly confesses.

"Do you believe him? About Mason wanting to find things out about me, but that he is not going to tell Mason what he finds out?" Kayla asks Kelly one last question.

"Actually, I do believe him. I felt his emotions and intentions, and they were genuine. Whatever they have planned, they are trying to fill you in about it, without Mason knowing. I think the next time he comes in, and he will be back, you should let him in and see what he has to say. I mean, what could it hurt?" Kelly finishes as she turns and walks towards one of the white walls, unseen by the naked eye, and slides behind it, and she is gone.

About the Author

Robert Starnes is not only the author of *The Multifamily Housing Guide Series: Leasing 101 - Garden Style*, and *The Saving History Series: Time Keeper*, and *School Bound*, but he is also the publisher. He created Starnes Books LLC so that he could have full control over his work and to be able to help other self-publish authors with free advice on what they can do to save money and not be taken advantage of for their hard work.

After being diagnosed with Asperger's Syndrome, which it is now part of a broader category called ASD (Autism Spectrum Disorder), at the age of 43, things started to click with him. After being able to identify and manage the parts of ASD he had, he was able to hone in on his creative writing. At a young age he did not like to read, because he had difficulty with the words on the pages in front of him. He knew the words and understood them, but his brain would comprehend them faster than his voice could speak them. This would cause him to either leave out words, or cause him to read very slowly so that he could have his eyes go back over the words again, two to three times, before his voice caught up with his brain. This embarrassment would stop him from reading for many years.

As an adult learning to face his fears, he began to read John Grisham novels. He loves the law and movies, so it was perfect for him to read the "The Last Juror" before watching the movie. After reading such a great novel then watching the movie, he quickly learned he enjoyed comparing the differences between the novels and the movies. That was all it took for him to begin to enjoy reading for the first time. For many years, he would only read novels that were going to become movies, because that was what he enjoyed about reading. After many years, he read another novel that became a movie, but they never completed the movie series. The novel was so good that he completed the book series, which in turn gave him a new enjoyment for reading without the novels becoming movies.

With this in Robert's mind, he has written his series for anyone that may be going through the same things he went through as a child, or adult, with reading, and is trying to find a way for them to connect with the world of reading. He believes that you can read and write a perfectly great action-packed novel that does not have to be 800 pages thick to be accomplished. He believes giving someone the opportunity and a way to enter the world of reading, then that's the accomplishment. No one should be afraid to read or write in their own style for others to be able to want to read. His mind does not work the same as a traditional writer's does and retains things much more than another person's may, so you will not find very much repeating, or recapping, in his series. You will find action, adventure, and history from the very first chapter to the very end.

To Robert, everyone is different and unique, and should be celebrated every day for being just who they are. He finds that when life may get you down, you can always get away in your own imagination with the help of a good book.

He was born in Texas, but now does most of his writing in Alabama. To learn more about him and his books, visit starnesbooksllc.com, or follow @Starnes_Books on twitter, and find @starnesbooksllc on Instagram.

Books by Robert Starnes

Saving History Series

Time Keeper – Starnes Books LLC (2018)
School Bound – Starnes Books LLC (2019)
Search Begins – Starnes Books LLC (2019)
Loose Ends – Starnes Books LLC (2019)
Final Hour – Starnes Books LLC (2021)

The Multifamily Housing Guide Series

Leasing 101: Garden Style – Starnes Books, LLC (2018)

The Multifamily Housing Guide – Leasing 101 Garden Style Edition – Lulu's publishing (2016 retired print)

Books Published by Starnes Books LLC

***Novel Study – Time Keeper** – Patricia Carpenter (2018)*
***Trip of a Lifetime** – Eric K. Reinholt (2020)*